TEXAS TORNADO

Every gunhawk in the great South-west knew the legend—
everyone except the masked outlaw who boarded the gold-
laden Sunset Limited and laced two bullets through Ranger
Tom Shafer's heart.

Determined to have revenge, Jim Hatfield, the Ranger's ace
man, strapped on his Colts and rode into the Big Bend
country to bring back the murderer—dead or alive!

But soon the savage chase became a bloody battle between
land-hungry farmers and defiant cowmen whose destiny
could never be decided until Shafer's killer and the steel-
nerved Hatfield met—gun to gun!

TEXAS TORNADO

Jackson Cole

GUNSMOKE

This hardback edition 2007
by BBC Audiobooks Ltd
by arrangement with
Golden West Literary Agency

ISBN 13: 978 1 405 68100 1

British Library Cataloguing in Publication Data available.

Printed and bound in Great Britain by
Antony Rowe Ltd., Chippenham, Wiltshire

CHAPTER I

THE RIO GRANDE is a strange river. Rising in the San Juan Mountains of southwestern Colorado, it flows eastward eighty miles as a mountain stream, then enters the San Luis Valley where its course changes to south. It crosses into New Mexico through the Rio Grande Canyon. Across the state its course is through a series of arid basins and canyons cut in the tranverse ridges, the last of which are El Paso Canyon and El Paso Valley. From the latter point to its mouth, the river forms the boundary, a continually shifting boundary, between Texas and Mexico.

Essentially a storm water stream subject to great and sudden floods, the Rio Grande is startling in the extreme fluctuations of its volume. The river may be dry at El Paso when its lower course is overflowing its banks. The stream is often referred to as a mile wide and a foot deep, too thin to plow and too thick to drink. But the description does not hold good when the Rio de las Palmas is in flood, a raging torrent flowing 600,000 cubic feet a second.

Jim Hatfield, standing on the foredeck of the steamboat *Ranchero,* pondered the river's erratic behavior as he watched the old stern-wheeler butt her stubby prow into the churning yellow waves. The *Ranchero* was flat-bottomed and of shallow draught. But she was powerfully engined and made good progress against the current.

It was seldom that the big steamboat ever followed the course of the river this far west. Usually, Laredo or Del Rio was about her upstream limit. More often she nosed around Rio Grande City and Brownsville, and from there to the mouth of the river.

This trip was out of the ordinary. She had been chartered at Del Rio by a group of emigrating farmers for a trip to the east rincon of the Big Bend. At Dawes Landing, friends with wagons would meet them and transport them to their new homes in the northern reaches of the Bend. Their goods had already been sent overland via covered wagon. The voices of women and children mingled with the steady "bat-bat" of the paddles and the cheerful "chow-chow" of the exhaust.

Hatfield glanced toward the aft deck where Goldy, his big sorrel, stood in a stall constructed of heavy planks. He looked toward the low hills a quarter of a mile to the north.

"Funny," he mused, "there's a jigger on horseback over on the lower slopes who's been pacing us all afternoon. Wonder why he's so darn interested in this old flat-bottom? Of course, he may be just a chuck-line riding cowhand taking it easy. But he sure has been keeping an eye on us."

At the same moment, Hatfield himself was under discussion. The captain and mate of the steamer stood near the rail and talked together in low tones.

"He's a salty lookin' hombre, that big cowboy," said the captain, a wizened oldtimer. "Look at the way them guns is slung. A two-gun, quick-draw man or I miss my guess. 'Pears to pack influence somewhere. When he come aboard at Del Rio, he had a letter from Kennedy, the owner, orderin' us to build a pen for that yaller horse. He's gettin' off at Dawes Landin', same as the farmers."

The fierce light of the setting sun etched the sternly handsome profile of the man named Hatfield, an old Lieutenant of the Rangers, sometimes called the Lone Wolf. Much more than six feet tall, his girth matched his height. His lean hawk face was dominated by long, black-lashed eyes of a peculiar shade of green. His rather wide mouth, grin-quirked at the corners, somewhat relieved the tinge of fierceness evinced by the high-bridged nose above and the grimly square chin beneath. Beneath his pushed back "J.B." there was hair so black a blue shadow seemed to lie upon it. He wore the careless garb of the rangeland —overalls, batwing chaps, faded blue shirt and vivid handker-chief looped about his throat—and he wore it as Richard the Lionhearted must have worn armor. About his lean waist were double cartridge belts. From the carefully worked and oiled cut-out holsters protruded the black butts of heavy guns.

"Chances are he's just a cowhand movin' from one ranch to another," the mate replied to the Captain's remark. "Kennedy is always anxious to please the cattlemen. Most of the business his boats do comes from them, you know."

"Reckon that's right," the Captain agreed. "Guess I'm just jumpy, with nigh onto a hundred thousand dollars in specie in the cabin. That's the real reason for this trip, you know. Takin' the farmers is just a sort of blind. Kennedy learned they were headin' for the Bend and made 'em an attractive offer. The bank figgers shippin' the dinero this way is a smart move, considerin' the trouble they been havin' on the railroad and the stages of late."

"May not be so smart when they're packin' it from the Landin' up into the Bend," observed the mate.

"Oh, nobody would think of lookin' in a farm wagon for anything to steal," deprecated the Captain. "And the shipment's been kept a dead secret."

"Don't anything seem to be kept a secret in this darn country of late," the mate grunted pessimistically. "Well, we should make the Landin' before midnight, and unload in the mornin'. After that, it's no concern of ours. Just the same, though, I'm keepin' my gun handy."

"Me, too," agreed the Captain, "and Pedro is on the lookout, too. And that shuck pilot is something to go up against."

"I'm more scared of him than anything else," grunted the mate, with his usual gloom. "Did you ever see such a face! But he sure knows every snag and sandbank in this darn river, and where the channel is all the time. He's took a course up river like a snake through a cactus patch and ain't grounded once."

The sun was low in the west and the yellow flood of the Rio Grande was shot with glimmers of gold and bloody scarlet. Purple shadows were climbing the lower slopes of the hills to the north. Their crests were ringed about with saffron flame. To the south, the multi-colored mountains of Mexico glowed and smoldered in the dying light.

Absently noting the beauty of the scene, Hatfield mused on the details of the grim tragedy that provided the reason for his being on the old flat-bottom plowing up the Rio Grande.

Young Tom Shafer was a Texas Ranger, and very, very proud of it. He hadn't been a Ranger for long—only about three months—but he was fired with the Ranger spirit and steeped in the traditions of the famous corps.

As he sat in the daycoach of the speeding Sunrise Limited, Tom Shafer thought of his coming meeting with Captain Bill McDowell, to whose command he had been assigned. He gazed out of the window, a smile on his fresh young fighter's face.

To the south was the Big Bend country, a land of strange legends and stirring deeds. Situated there were the mysterious, multi-colored Chisos Mountains, the home of outlaw bands. There, too, was the Comanche Trail which Indians once used to raid into Mexico, but which now was used more frequently by smugglers and owlhoots. The Caballo Mountains, Maravillas Creek, Mule Ear Peaks, Boquillas Pass, the Picotera Mountains, where, tradition says, is the famous Lost Nigger Mine, were all in the Big Bend—names of adventure, romance and blood. And beyond was the awful gorge that is the Grand Canyon of Santa.

Helena, where the Rio Grande thunders between towering walls of stone, between the confines of which birds have been known to start because they were unable to fly above the walls due to the terrific down draughts.

Tom Shafer hoped Captain McDowell might assign him to duty in the Big Bend, perhaps send him to search out and destroy the notorious Scarlet Riders, so named because of the flaming red handkerchiefs that they pierced with eye-holes and used for masks.

Young Tom was dreaming of his good fortune and the excitement to come when a screaming sound of tortured metal rocked the car as the brake shoes ground against the wheels. The day coach leaped and bucked as the heavy Pullmans behind crashed together. Passengers were hurled forward against the seats in front of them.

A splintering crash, a last terrific jolt and the train came to a halt. The passengers picked themselves up, yelling and swearing.

The front door banged open. A man strode into the coach. He was tall and broad. His hatbrim was pulled low. His face was swathed in a scarlet handkerchief pierced with eye-holes. He held a gun in each hand.

"Elevate!" he shouted in a deep, hoarse voice.

Tom Shafer was on his feet in the aisle when the man entered. He gazed squarely into the black muzzles of the leveled guns.

Through young Tom's mind flashed stories he had heard of Ranger daring in just such a situation, of winning out against seemingly insurmountable odds. But young Tom forgot that Ranger courage is accompanied by cool-headedness and sound judgment. Even Captain McDowell respected the barrel of a Forty-five trained in his direction. Under such circumstances, Captain Bill would sit tight and wait for a break.

Tom Shafer didn't sit tight. He went for his gun. Before it ·

cleared leather, he died—two bullets laced through his heart.

The bandit peered over his smoking Colt.

"Anybody else?" he inquired. "I aim to accommodate."

There was nobody else. The passengers stood rigid with horror, hands reaching for the roof.

Outside they heard a stutter of shots, then a roaring explosion. The train robbers had hurled a stick of dynamite against the express car door.

There were a few more shots, shouted commands, then several moments of silence shattered by another explosion that was immediately muffled by the walls of the express car.

Inside the car, as the smoke cleared, the big iron safe lay against the wall, its door sagging crazily from one hinge. Nearby lay the dead express messenger.

There was fifty thousand dollars in the safe. It didn't stay there long. A few minutes later it disappeared into the brush with the owlhoots.

Captain McDowell was at the station when the Limited, hours late, paused at Franton to unload its grisly cargo. As he looked down on the face of young Tom Shafer, his own craggy features were bleak as chiselled granite.

Tom Shafer's father had been a life-long friend of McDowell's. It had been McDowell who brought about young Tom's appointment to the Rangers.

"Thought I was doin' the boy a favor," McDowell muttered to himself sadly.

While repairs were being made to the pilot and engine front, smashed when the locomotive plowed into the mass of stone and logs heaped on the track by the bandits, Captain McDowell questioned passengers and crewmen, but with scant results. All agreed, however, that the masked robbers were the notorious Scarlet Riders. And that the very tall man who killed Tom Shafer was the leader of the band.

McDowell walked slowly back to his office. As he neared the

building which fronted to the north on the main street of the town, he suddenly uttered an exultant exclamation—

"Blazes! Knew he'd get in today or tomorrow, but the big jigger seems always to show up right when he's needed most. Hi yuh, Jim! Almighty glad to see you!"

The man riding across the way waved a greeting to the Ranger Captain. A moment later he dismounted with lithe grace and strode forward, leaving his magnificent golden sorrel horse securely tied to the evening breeze.

"How are you, suh?" Hatfield asked. "Anything wrong?"

"Plenty," grunted McDowell. "Come on into the office and I'll tell you about it. I'll send Chuck out to take care of Goldy."

In terse sentences, Captain McDowell told Hatfield about the robbery and killings on the Sunrise Limited.

Hatfield listened in silence. His face remained composed, but his eyes were as cold as a glacier lake under a stormy sky.

"Know anything about these jiggers you call the Scarlet Riders?" he asked when McDowell paused.

"Not over much," the commander of the Border Battalion replied. "They been swallerforkin' around the Bend for a while. Runnin' off some cows, holdin' up a stage, grabbin' one of the Terlingua quicksilver mine payrolls. Never anything real big till this train trobbery. Got their name from the red handkerchiefs they wear for masks."

"Where do they hang out?"

"That's a question," said McDowell. "Some folks say the Chisos Mountains. Others say they hole up in the Carmens down in Mexico. My notion is the Del Nortes or the Santiagos, west of Marton. That's hole-in-the-wall country for fair. That gives 'em a natural sweep into the Marathon Basin, which is one of the oldest sedimentary formations on the North American Continent. The peaks to the west and south used to be Indian lookouts, and I reckon the owlhoots put 'em to the same use nowadays. Plenty of cows in the Marathon, and on the Tobso

Flats to the east. Mines in the Chisos, with stage routes runnin' to 'em. Plenty of pickin's for a salty bunch with savvy."

"What kind of local enforcement officers over there?"

"Always been pretty good. The sheriff of the county is okay, and I reckon he got re-elected today. Haven't heard the result of the returns, yet, but the county has always been safe for the regular party."

Captain McDowell paused again. Hatfield gazed at him expectantly, but in silence. The Captain tugged his mustache, hesitated, seemed to make a resolve.

"I'm always in the notion to leave such mavericks to the local authorities so far as possible," he resumed slowly. "Usually they don't amount to anything a good sheriff can't handle. We've got enough to do without skalleyhootin' after every stray cow widelooper who shows up. But what happened today on the train sort of changes the picture."

McDowell paused again to stuff tobacco into his pipe. He got the pipe going well, and blew out a cloud of smoke.

"That chore down on the Border I wired you about can't wait, Jim," he said. "Captain Brooks is expectin' you and needs you and the boys. It may take considerable time, but after it's cleaned up, suppose you amble up into the Bend and give things a once-over. Okay?"

Hatfield nodded. "Always heard it was nice country," he remarked.

"Huh!" snorted the Captain. "Nice for horned toads and sidewinders! There's hellions in that section ornery enough to eat off the same plate with a snake!"

The Lone Wolf looked pleased.

CHAPTER II

Hatfield raised his glance to the pilot house. He waved his hand, and smiled. He had taken a liking to the young Mexican pilot, despite his remarkable and somewhat unprepossessing appearance.

Pedro was tall and lean, slender with the slenderness of a rapier blade. His dark face was seamed and puckered with the scars of knife wounds. He had a long, drooping nose set very much to one side over his thin-lipped mouth. His eyes were unusual, to say the least. Due to old knife work, one eyelid hung continually lower than the other, lending to his otherwise sinister face a droll and unexpected impishness.

Pedro waved back to the tall Ranger, one eye glowering, the other leering, while his crooked but very white teeth flashed in a grin.

Hatfield walked over to where the captain stood by the rail.

"Understand you figure to make the Landing during the night, suh," he remarked.

"That's right," the captain agreed. "At the rate we're goin', we had ought to make it by ten or eleven o'clock. Then we'll tie up and unload in the mornin'."

"If you don't mind, suh, I'll unload as soon as we tie up," Hatfield answered. "Got a long ride ahead of me, and it's cooler at night this time of the year."

13

"Okay," the captain agreed. "I'll drop the gangplank for you."

The sun went down in a riot of scarlet and gold. The flaming sky dimmed to cold gray that swiftly deepened to velvety black. The stars came out, looking like grapes of light that seemed to brush the hilltops. The broad band of the flooded river became vague and elusive while the wave crests were flecked with phosphorescent fire. Pedro leaned over the wheel, peering ahead with his mismated eyes and deftly twirling the spokes as he sought out the channel.

A couple of hours after sunset Hatfield helped Goldy to a hefty portion of oats, gave him a rubdown and got the rig on him.

"Want to be all ready to hit the trail as soon as we tie up," he told the sorrel. "I've a notion a stretching will be good for your legs. But being lucky enough to get this ride on the boat up from Del Rio sure saved you considerable trompin'!"

Another hour passed and Hatfield estimated that they were only a few miles south of Dawes Landing, the point of disembarkation. He lounged close to Goldy's stall, smoking a cigarette and thinking deeply.

Without warning it happened. There was a terrific crash, a grinding and jolting. The boat came to a stop as if gripped by a giant hand. Everyone standing was hurled headlong to the deck. Hatfield heard Pedro's bellowed oaths. The exhaust snapped off. The beat of the paddles ceased. The *Ranchero* swung crazily as the current gripped her. In the fore part of the boat burst an ominous glow that grew in intensity. Up the steel ladder, the half-breed stokers swarmed from the shallow engine room.

Half dazed by the shock of his fall, Hatfield scrambled to his feet. Inside the stall, Goldy snorted and squealed, but apparently had not been hurt.

"Pedro slipped up," Hatfield muttered, rubbing his bruised

head. "Must have hit a sandbank or a submerged ledge. Sounded like it ripped her whole bow out. Good gosh! everybody is going loco!"

The boat was a sea of confusion. People were running to and fro, shouting and screaming. The captain was bellowing for order. Pedro's curses rose high above the tumult.

Something bumped and grated against the *Ranchero's* side. At first, Hatfield thought they had grounded on a ledge. But then he saw a man scramble over the rail. He had a gun in his hand, a mask of red cloth across his face. After him came another and another.

As Hatfield stared in astonishment, a gun cracked. The captain yelled with pain and reeled sideways, clutching at his blood-spouting arm.

"Elevate!" roared the gun-wielder. "The first hellion to make a move gets it. Stop that damn yellin'!"

Jim Hatfield made a move. His hands streaked down and up. Both his Colts let go with a rippling crash.

The first gunman hurtled back as if a huge fist had crashed into his chest. He hit the rail, spun across it and plunged into the water. A second man went down, kicking and clawing on the deck. Over the rail surged three more masked men, shooting as they came.

Fire spurted from the pilot house. One of the newcomers went back over the rail. The captain picked up his fallen gun with his left hand and fired away at the owlhoots. Hatfield's sixes boomed again, and another man went down. The others retreated over the rail. Hatfield heard their boots thud on the bottom of the boat in which they had come. He bounded forward, stuffing fresh cartridges into his empty guns.

From the river bank sounded the boom of a rifle. A heavy slug whined past Hatfield's head. He whirled, leaped to Goldy's stall and snatched his Winchester from the saddle boot. He sent a stream of lead hissing toward shadowy forms on the river bank. Answering bullets stormed about him, kicked splinters from the deck and thudded against the pilot house.

Then the current gripped the *Ranchero* with full force and hurled her toward the middle of the river. In a moment they were sweeping downstream and out of range.

Hatfield ran to the wounded captain.

"Hurt much?" he asked.

"Just a hole through the meat. I'll be all right," the captain gasped. "Tie it up in a minute."

"Do you know what this is all about?" Hatfield urged.

"Money shipment in the cabin. They were after it, and didn't get it, thanks to you, cowboy. They—good God, the boat's afire!"

It was. Flames crackled and roared in the *Ranchero's* bow.

"Oil and bacon up there," said the captain. "We'll never get it out. Pedro!" he bellowed. "Head her for the shore, and hold her there! We gotta unload."

Pedro was jangling the engine-room bell madly.

"Power!" he bawled back. "Give me power! How can I steer without power! Get the engines going!"

The captain lurched to the engine-room hatch, wringing the blood from his fingers. No answer came to his repeated orders. The *Ranchero* continued to drift and spin. The flames leaped higher. The screams of frightened women, the crying of children and the shouts of men rose in a bedlam of horrid sound.

Hatfield shouldered the captain aside. He dropped down the steel-runged ladder to the floor of the engine room. Instantly two things caught his eye. One was a film of water sloshing over the floor. The other was the crumpled and unconscious form of the engineer. He was bleeding from a wound just above his right eye.

"Butted his head into something when she hit, and knocked himself out," Hatfield muttered.

With no apparent effort, he lifted the engineer's heavy form and draped it over his shoulder. With the water sloshing over his boots, he strode to the ladder and mounted it. Reaching the deck he laid the unconscious man on the boards.

"Look after him," he told the captain and the mate. He turned, shouted to the pilot, "Pedro, can you hold her against the bank till the passengers get off?"

"*Si, Capitan,*" Pedro shouted back. "As soon as I find a point low enough. Give me power, and I'll hold her till I burn!"

"Good man!" Hatfield called. "You'll get the power."

He dropped down the ladder again. A glance told him the water was rising. From the bow came an angry glow. The fire had already eaten through the deck boards. Smoke was swirling about, and growing thicker.

Hatfield opened the throttle, cautiously. Instantly the great cranks began to turn. The huge arms leading to the paddle wheel began to rise and fall. The steady beat of the paddles sounded. He widened the throttle, and felt the boat answer to the wheel as Pedro twirled the spokes.

But the steam was falling rapidly. He flung open the furnace door and heaved in billets of oil-soaked wood. The flames roared. He closed the door and opened the blower wide to secure a forced draught. Another moment and he flung in more wood. He glanced at the water glass, saw that the water was dangerously low. But steam pressure was the great need now. He'd have to take a chance on burning the boiler and causing an explosion that would blow the engine room and himself to Mexico. Anxiously he watched the needle of the steam gauge rise. It reached the pressure limit. The safety valve opened with a hiss and roar.

But Hatfield realized that Pedro was having trouble. The mighty current of the swollen Rio Grande was forcing the clumsy boat toward midstream.

"Got to have more power," he muttered.

Reaching up, he shoved the weight on the safety valve arm

to the last notch. Then he picked up a heavy wrench and hung that on the end of the arm. Grimly, he watched the needle waver past the safety mark.

The *Ranchero* answered to the accelerated beat of the paddles. Hatfield felt her nose come about.

He felt something else, too. The sting of sparks showering down on him through the open hatch. The fire was sweeping back. Any moment, flames might cut off his only exit from the smoke-filled, water logged engine room.

Steam was hissing from the ash pan where the water was creeping in over the hot coals. At this rate, it would soon be high enough to drown the fire in the furnace.

Batting out the sparks that smouldered his shirt, Hatfield went back to stoking the furnace. In the pilot house above, with flame and smoke wreathing about him, Pedro twirled the spokes and cursed the day he was born.

Hatfield was almost thrown off balance by a sudden jar. The *Ranchero's* stern swung around. The paddles churned the water madly. Pedro had nosed her against the bank and was holding her there at a sharp angle. Hatfield heard the bang and rattle of the lowered gangplank, and a thud of feet racing across the deck. He tried the last water gauge cock, and got a hiss of dry steam.

"Liable to let go any minute," he muttered, glancing at the still rising steam gauge needle.

A tongue of flame flickered over the hatch opening, withdrew, and flickered again. Smoke billowed down, causing Hatfield to cough and strangle. Once more the glowing tongue of flame writhed over the opening. This time it did not withdraw altogether. Hatfield watched it grimly, turned and hurled more wood into the furnace.

Suddenly he was aware of a lessening of the noise above-decks. He felt the *Ranchero* swing around, lurch, begin to move swiftly.

A voice called down to him through the hatchway. "Come, *Capitan,* come! All are ashore! Come quickly!"

Hatfield hurried up the ladder. The hot rungs scorched his hands. He gasped as he went through the welter of flame and smoke that blanketed the opening. An instant later, he was on deck, beating out the fire that smouldered his clothes. Beside him was Pedro, burned and blackened, but with one eye leering roguishly. The *Ranchero* was hurtling downstream, her whole forepart a welter of flame.

Hatfield raced to Goldy's pen. He flung down the bars, led the shivering horse from the stall and swung into the saddle.

"Up behind me," he told Pedro. "We'll let Goldy take us out. We'll unfork and swim soon as we hit the water."

Pedro clambered up behind the cantle and gripped Hatfield around the waist. The Lone Wolf's voice rang out—

"Take it, feller! Trail!"

Goldy soared over the rail like a bird on the wing and hit the water far out from the side of the careening boat. Instantly Hatfield and Pedro slipped from his back. When they broke surface, Hatfield veered Goldy's nose to the left and they set out at a long slant for the north bank, breasting the current with strong strokes. Far ahead, the *Ranchero* roared downstream, spouting flame and smoke like a volcano.

"She won't last long," Hatfield mutttered.

At that instant, a tremendous explosion blew the *Ranchero* to pieces. Flaming timbers hurtled through the air, struck the water with hissing splashes and vanished from view. Darkness descended on the yellow water.

"Just in time," Hatfield shouted to Pedro. "We'd have taken a long trip to somewhere if we'd still been on her."

Pedro gulped a reply, and after that they saved their breath for the struggle with the river.

CHAPTER III

THE CURRENT WAS STRONG, and they were swept a long way downstream before they sloshed through the shallows and sank exhausted on a stretch of sandy beach.

For several minutes they lay resting. Then they emptied the water from their boots, wrung out their clothes as best they could and climbed the bank to the prairie above.

"We'll ride upstream till we run onto the others," Hatfield decided. "You say they all got ashore?"

"Every one," Pedro replied.

"You did a fine chore, feller, holding her against the bank all that time," Hatfield congratulated his companion. "It must have been almighty hot in that wheel house."

"*Si*," Pedro agreed, "it was. But," he added dryly, "I could escape whenever it got too hot, which was more than you could do from that engine room if the deck had fallen in."

"Was too darn busy to think about it," Hatfield chuckled as they cantered westward over the prairie. "Say," he exclaimed a few minutes later, "don't I see fires ahead?"

"*Si*," Pedro agreed. "The farmers have made camp on the bank."

They rode on toward the winking fires. They were a few hundred yards distant when a deep, harsh voice challenged them from the shadows of a clump of thicket—

20

"Halt!"

Hatfield pulled Goldy to a stop, "Okay, feller," he called. "Look us over. I'm coming ahead, slow."

"Come ahead," the other replied, "but don't try no tricks. I got a bead on you, and I don't miss."

Hatfield paced Goldy slowly toward the thicket. A moment more and a lank farmer stepped from concealment, rifle in hand, peering forward.

"Praise the Lord for His mercies!" he suddenly boomed. "Both of you alive! We never expected to see either of you again. Come on to camp and let the folks thank you for what you did."

"Everybody okay?" Hatfield asked as he shook hands with the farmer.

"Everybody's fine," the other replied. "All got ashore without as much as a burn. We even packed along most all of our blankets and other truck, includin' gunny sacks of coffee and bacon and corn pone. Reckon you fellers could stand a few cups, steamin' hot. You look a mite damp and chilly. Come on. Abner Hatch is holed up in that other brush heap over there, keepin' an eye on things down this way. We ain't takin' no chances with those onery galoots, though I reckon they got a bellyful."

The hardy farmers, accustomed to taking misadventure in their stride, had already set up a comfortable camp on the river bank. The children were asleep on blanket-beds. The women, of the same stern stock as the husbands and fathers, were cooking over the fires.

Hatfield and Pedro were greeted with enthusiasm. After several cups of coffee, some crisply fried bacon and corn pone, Hatfield sought the captain of the *Ranchero*.

The captain's bullet-punctured arm was swathed in bandages, but he otherwise appeared little the worse for wear.

"Did you get the dinero ashore?" Hatfield asked him.

"Every last sack," the captain chuckled. "It was considerable of a chore—ninety thousand dollars in gold is a mite hefty—

but we did it. The farmers pitched in and helped. They're a cool lot, them fellers. They sloshed water on the fire, smokin' their pipes and takin' it as easy as if they were at a picnic. Packed most all of their truck ashore with 'em, too. I figure they didn't hardly leave a blanket or a skillet behind."

"They're of the breed that made this country what it is," Hatfield returned gravely.

"Reckon that's so," the captain agreed. "And I reckon, too," he added, "that them Scarlet Riders got thir come-uppance proper for once. Two of 'em went into the water, and I don't figure they come up again. Three more, or what was left of 'em, got roasted along with the boat. I've a notion you plugged one on the bank with your rifle, judgin' from the way he squalled."

Hatfield eyed the captain. "The Scarlet Riders?" he repeated.

"That's right," the captain said. "I saw the red masks they were wearin'. That's the bunch what has been operatin' in the upper Bend. I heard about 'em my last trip up this way. They're the bunch that robbed the Sunrise Limited on Election Day and killed a Texas Ranger. They always wear red masks. That's how they got their name. A bad bunch, all right. And son, they'll sure be lookin' for you, that is if they got a line on you tonight or learn later it was you who busted up their little try for the Terlingua Mine money."

Hatfield nodded. However, he was inclined to discount the captain's notion that the Scarlet Riders of the upper Bend were responsible for the attack on the *Ranchero*. Hatfield knew that wearing a distinctive badge of some sort was an old owlhoot trick, designed to frighten their prospective victims. He also knew that once a band has acquired such a reputation, imitators spring up quickly. He suspected that the owlhoots who attacked the steamer were trading on the sinister reputation of the notorious Scarlet Riders.

"The real bunch in the upper Bend would hardly be working way over here, several days' ride from their hangout," he told himself. Aloud he remarked to the captain, "Wonder how they knew you were packing that dinero?"

"That's one I'd like to have answered," the captain growled. "Nobody but the bank, the Terlingua Mine and the boat line officials were supposed to know about it. But them blasted Scarlet Riders 'pear to know everything. What *I'd* like to know, too, is how come Pedro happened to hit that rock. He knows the river from one end to the other. Never knowed him to do a thing like that before."

Hatfield had his own explanation of the mystery, but he refrained from comment at the moment.

"Suppose the wagons will be at Dawes Landing waiting for the farmers to show up?" he observed.

"Uh-huh, reckon they will, and the wagon to pack the money up to the Terlingua, too," the captain replied. "They'll be wonderin' what happened when we don't show up come mornin'."

"We should be within ten miles of the Landing," Hatfield said. "As soon as it is light, I'll ride up there and tell them what happened. Then they can run the wagons down here and pick up their loads."

"That'll help a lot," the captain replied gratefully. "Reckon me and Pedro and the other boys can hire horses or rigs at the Dawes ranch to take us back to Del Rio."

"Wouldn't be surprised," Hatfield agreed. "Damn shame about the boat."

"Oh, Kennedy has plenty more of them old tubs," the captain replied. "Besides, she was insured. We saved the money, and nobody got hurt bad, which is the important thing. Well, my arm don't feel so good and I'm tired. I figger to try and knock off a mite of shuteye. The farmers are keepin' watch."

Hatfield decided he would get some sleep too. After making sure that Goldy was given a good rubdown, and left grazing contentedly nearby, he rolled up in a borrowed blanket beside one of the fires and slept soundly till dawn.

He was in the saddle shortly after daybreak, however, and riding west along the river bank.

For several miles he rode slowly, scanning the turbulent water. He was perhaps three miles above the site of the camp when he pulled Goldy to a halt and stared at a swirling body of water fifty yards or so out from the bank.

That miniature rapid said plainly that directly beneath the surface was a submerged ledge. Hatfield could even see the glimmer of the dark stone as the water rolled over it.

"That's what we hit, all right," he muttered. "But how come it was right where those hellions were waiting? Smack in mid-channel, too. Pedro must have known about it. Something funny about this."

He rode closer and gazed down the shelving bank. Plain to see was the high water mark, several feet above the present level of the river's surface. And Hatfield knew that the waters of the Rio Grande had not receded for a week.

Turning, he looked upstream. About a hundred yards distant the river made a sharp bend. The north shore was on the outside of the curve.

Hatfield rode on until he reached the bend. Suddenly he uttered a sharp exclamation, and pulled Goldy to a halt.

At the apex of the curve was a sand pit that extended outward for a score of feet. From the tip of the pit ran a line of rough cribbing built of stout tree trunks and filled with boulders. Hatfield gave a low whistle.

"Plenty of savvy," he exclaimed aloud. "Uh-huh, that bunch have wrinkles on their horns, all right. Built that cribbing out into the stream at just the right angle to shunt the current away from the channel and toward the middle of the river. Before the water could overcome the eddy set up by the abrupt change of direction, the full flow was beyond that underwater ledge. As a consequence, the water in the channel is lowered considerably where it passes over the reef. And what Pedro always knew to be a safe crossing has been changed so that that jagged ledge would rip the bottom out of even a shallow draught boat like the *Ranchero*. Of all the smart tricks! Somebody had to know his mathematics and engineering principles to figure the proper angle to set that cribbing. This *is* getting interesting."

Hatfield rode westward at a fast clip.

Dawes Landing had once been the site of a military post during the wars with the Indians. Now it was a huddle of shacks and false-fronts. It accommodated the scattered ranches of the section, the largest and most prosperous being the spread that gave the settlement its name. There was a Mexican town across the river and the Landing was a minor port of entry. It was more than a "minor" port for the smuggling industry, Hatfield shrewdly surmised, the Comanche Trail being not far off.

There was unwonted activity around the Landing that morning. On the outskirts of the settlement were clustered a dozen huge covered wagons. Attending them were a group of bronzed and bearded farmers. Hatfield rode up to the wagons and called the farmers together. In terse sentences he related the *Ranchero's* mishap and relayed the message sent by its passengers. The farmers listened in silence until the tale was finished. Their leader, a lanky individual with a brown face that did not move a muscle, scrutinized Hatfield keenly, fingering his grizzled beard the while.

"It's a funny soundin' yarn," he observed frankly, "but you look to be a reg'lar sort of feller, even though you are a cowhand. And the boat didn't get here last night as she was supposed to, that's sure for certain. Reckon you're dealin' straight with us. We'll hitch up and drive down there."

Hatfield received the comment with a smile. He understood the people he was dealing with.

"You say the fellers who attacked the boat wore red handkerchiefs over their faces?" the old man commented. "Well, I reckon they *might* have been them Scarlet Riders fellers we've heard so much about."

Hatfield had no trouble picking out the Terlingua Mine wagon sent to fetch the gold shipment. The driver and hands were dressed much the same as the others, but in demeanor they differed from the stolid, methodical farmers. They were alert, keen-eyed men who looked very capable.

After the farmers departed to hitch up, the driver drew Hatfield aside.

"Did the boat manage to unload her cargo?" he asked casually.

"The really valuable part," Hatfield replied.

The driver nodded. "Then we'll mosey down there, too," he announced understanding the Lone Wolf perfectly. He fingered his chin a moment and shot Hatfield a shrewd glance.

"Them grangers," he remarked, with a hitch of his thumb toward the other wagons, "they don't believe it was the Scarlet Riders who tackled to boat. They figure it was just another trick of the big ranchers to make trouble. What do you think?"

"Doesn't look reasonable, does it?" Hatfield said. "No matter how much the ranchers may hate the farmers, I don't think they'd attempt what might have been wholesale murder," Hatfield countered.

"Guess you're right," the other replied soberly. "You say the crew fought 'em off?"

"That's right," Hatfield replied.

"Well, they must have done a good job of fightin'," declared the other. "Hope we're done with the sidewinders, but I figure we ain't. They evidently know just what's goin' on, and they'll make another try for that gold if they get half a chance. I'll bet on that."

"You fellers roll down from the upper Bend with the farmers?" Hatfield asked.

"That's right."

"What excuse did you give for joining up with them?"

"To pick up a load of minin' machinery the boat would unload," the teamster replied.

"The mine ever do that before?"

"Not that I ever heard tell of," the other admitted.

Hatfield regarded him curiously. "Well," he said, "it looks to me as if you might just as well have painted letters on your wagon a foot high tellin' folks what you were coming down here for. Especially since you're using a light wagon totally different from those big covered wains."

The teamster shot Hatfield a startled look. He tugged hard at the lobe of his left ear. "Dad blame it!" he growled querulously. "Now you got me plumb worried. I've a notion everybody knows what we'll be packin'."

"Well, it's pretty well advertised," Hatfield agreed dryly. "All the farmers down there and the boat crew know what's in those sacks. The captain had to tell them so they'd help pack 'em ashore."

The teamster swore explosively. "Sure looks like we're up against it," he growled. He tugged his ear again and was silent for a moment. "I got an idea," he said slowly. "The wagon train will be purty certain to make camp here at the Landin' tonight. Gettin' down to where the farmers are, loadin' up and rollin' back, they won't hardly more'n make the Landin' today."

"That's reasonable," Hatfield agreed. "What about it?"

"Just this," the teamster explained. "Us fellers will unhitch and make camp with 'em. But soon as it comes dark, we'll hitch up again and skalleyhoot north as fast as we can. If them blasted owlhoots are figurin' on makin' a try for the money, they'll hardly do it between here and where the farmers are campin' down the river. I figure if they make a try, it'll be after we turn west this side of Persimmon Gap, the pass northeast of the Santiagos. The farmers will keep on headin' north to the Gap. The trail to Terlingua turns west just south of the Gap.

Those robbin' gents will figure us to travel with the farmers' train. They'll follow the train to where we turn. If we can slide on ahead, we'll throw 'em plumb off."

Hatfield considered. "It might work, if they aren't keeping too close a watch on the train," he admitted. "Anyhow, separating from the train will remove the chance of the women and kids maybe getting hurt if a real shindig busts loose."

"That's right, too," nodded the teamster. "Uh-huh, I figure it's worth a try."

"Your light wagon should make good time along the Comanche Trail," Hatfield remarked. "If the owlhoots don't tumble to what's up before the train reaches the Gap, you should have a start that will get you in the clear. Yes, I reckon it's worth trying. But if the sidewinders catch on, well—"

He left the sentence unfinished. The teamster looked uncomfortable, and tugged at his ear.

"You ridin' back to the camp?" he asked suddenly.

Hatfield shook his head. "No, I'm heading north. Got a chore to attend to," he replied.

The other favored him with a long look. "Okay," he said. "Got to be rollin' now. There go the other wagons. *Adios.*"

"*Hasta Luego,*" Hatfield returned the Spanish good-bye. He turned Goldy's head and rode north by west, toward the Comanche Trail. The driver watched him out of sight.

"*Hasta Luego,*" he repeated thoughtfully. "That don't mean good-bye in Mex talk. That means 'till we meet again'!"

CHAPTER IV

THE SUN WAS BLAZING above the western peaks when Hatfield turned into the Comanche Trail. For some moments he sat his horse and gazed southward along the ancient track that glowed like a river of blood in the lurid light.

And blood was a fitting color, he knew well. By way of the ominous track, the fierce Plains Indians had raided south from Horsehead Crossing on the Pecos River, past Comanche Springs to the Comanche Crossing on the Rio Grande. The Comanches called September "the Mexican moon," for regularly in that month they came down from their strongholds for an invasion beyond the Rio Grande. They murdered and robbed, laid waste to a great no-man's land on both sides of the river. They burned the scant grassland to flush game until only cacti survived.

Here, too, slunk the Mescalero Apaches, the Cat People, mewing beneath the moon, with the *Andastes,* their sinister priesthood, in their grotesque masks of wolf and panther and bear, ranging right and left to scout the Trail. Here was the Dark Empire of the Tribes, over which they ruled supreme. Not until they inaugurated the presidio system, the chain of forts from Durango, Mexico, north, were the Spaniards able to hold the lands.

After the Indians came others as bad or even worse than the

aborigines. Smuggler, rustler, and robber used the Comanche and the adjacent Smuggler Trail, and still used them.

Hatfield knew that the wagon train would use the Comanche north to the farming country, passing through Persimmon Gap, the only pass through the Santiago chain.

But south of Persimmon Gap the treasure wagon must turn west to reach the mines.

"And somewhere between the Comanche and Terlingua the try for the gold will be made, if it's made at all," the Lone Wolf told Goldy. "That's one godawful country over there, where anything can happen. It's made to order for owlhoots who know it. Wish I knew it better. Well, we'll play our hunch and hope for the breaks. That's all we can do."

Turning the sorrel's head he rode northward for a good part of the night before he made camp under an overhung cliff. The morning light shone on the high notch in the towering rampart of the Santiagos through which the Comanche Trail ran to the level lands beyond.

After eating a sketchy breakfast from the provisions in his saddle pouch, Hatfield rode north again to where the trail began to climb the slopes to the notch. Here he sat his horse for a few minutes; then he turned west into a narrower track that snaked its way between steep slopes and low hills. He followed the trail for about two miles, then abruptly turned off to the south. He sent Goldy up a slope that ended in a bench that curved around the breast of the hills. Overhanging cliffs and bristles of growth rendered a rider on the bench almost invisible from the trail below.

Hatfield found a suitable spot and holed up in comfort. The bench was in easy rifle range of the trail.

"Sort of made to order," he mused.

The sun climbed the long slant of the eastern sky. Gradually the dark shadow of the mountains retreated until the track below lay shimmering in golden light. On into the east it stretched, silent and deserted.

Hatfield began to grow acutely uneasy. It seemed to him that the treasure wagon should have put in an appearance before now. He wondered if he had slipped up. Perhaps the attempt had been made somewhere between the trail fork and Dawes Landing. But then again, perhaps the wagoneers had decided to roll with the train.

And then, when he was just about ready to regain the trail and head back south on the Comanche, he sensed movement far to the east.

A faint yellow shimmer stained the crystal-clear air beyond a distant rise. He quickly catalogued it as dust kicked up by moving hoofs.

"Looks a trifle too heavy for the wagon," he told himself. "And moving too fast, too. Now what in blazes, I wonder?"

The yellow mist boiled steadily forward. Hatfield kept his eyes glued on the crest of the distant rise. Suddenly he uttered an exclamation.

Over the rise streamed a number of charging figures, dust swirling above them. Quickly, Hatfield identified them as horses traveling fast. They dipped down the sag, vanished for a few minutes in the hollow below, then reappeared. Hatfield counted seven mounted men.

"Those jiggers, whoever they are, 'pear to be in a hustle to get somewhere," he told Goldy.

On came the hurrying riders. They swept around the base of the swell below the bench, clicked past where Hatfield lay in concealment and vanished from sight to the west.

Jim Hatfield did some hard and fast thinking. Swiftly he debated his course of action. The speeding horsemen might be only a bunch of cowhands heading for some spread beyond the hills. That was perfectly possible, with the Dawes ranch and other holdings down around the river. If such was the case and he endeavoured to keep the riders in sight, he would be following a cold trail.

But he had an uneasy feeling that they could just as easily be the remainder of the bunch that attacked the steamer. If so where were they headed for, and why? The answer may be that they had seen through the teamster's ruse.

As Hatfield considered the problem with a concentration that approached mental agony, a second yellowish shimmer appeared above the distant ridge to the east. It was thinner than the first and traveled with less speed. With intense interest he watched it boil forward. His interest increased as a dark object bulged into view over the high crest. Quickly it resolved to a wagon drawn by eight horses. It was moving at a good speed.

Hatfield watched the wagon roll down the sag, vanish from sight in the hollow and appear once more. A few minutes more and it rumbled past his place of concealment, careened around the bulge and out of his range of vision.

"Let's go, feller," he told Goldy as he swung into the hull. "That's the money wagon, all right, and we've got to keep it in sight. If that bunch skalleyhootin' ahead do happen to be those hellions we're on the lookout for, they're liable to pull something any minute. Right now the advantage is all theirs. They can hole up anywhere ahead. But maybe we can hand them a mite of a surprise."

With the sorrel going at a fast clip, he rounded a bulge of cliff and again caught sight of the speeding wagon. For a mile he kept it in view. In view, also, was the trail ahead, stretching silent and deserted. Hatfield began to wonder if the riders he saw were not, after all, just a bunch of law-abiding cowhands.

And then, just as he was congratulating himself that everything was well under control, a new complication developed.

The bench that flowed along the breast of the hills continued unbroken, but gradually its contours changed. For some time the sag to the trail below had been increasing in steepness. Now it was almost a sheer cliff which a man, much less a horse, would be unable to negotiate. And the bench began to slope sharply inward, like the petal of a flower. Soon Hatfield found himself riding through a sort of lane of stone, with the trail below hidden from sight by the upward jut of stone that walled him in.

For a mile or more the "lane" continued, winding around the bulge of the cliffs. Hatfield increased Goldy's speed. He peered ahead and strained his ears to catch the rumble of the wagon.

Suddenly a stutter of shots sounded no great distance off. Hatfield swore as the firing continued for several moments, the cracking of six-guns punctuated by the heavier boom of rifles. Then abruptly as it had begun, the uproar ceased. Hatfield sent Goldy charging forward. To his relief, the wall on his right was lower, although the cliffs on his left continued unbroken. Another moment and he jerked Goldy to a slithering halt. He swore and glared ahead.

The wall that blocked his view had ended. But the bench had ended also. It had sluffed off to nothingness. Directly in front was a sheer drop of a hundred feet or more.

The trail lay within half a mile of the cliff face, curving westward to vanish from sight around a bulge. Speeding over its surface was the wagon. But now men rode on each side of the vehicle.

"The sidewinders put it over!" Hatfield growled. "I sure got myself properly outsmarted this time."

He whirled Goldy around and sent him racing back the way they had come. There was nothing to do but retrace his steps to a point where he could regain the trail below.

It seemed a very long time before he reached a spot where he could send the sorrel skalleyhooting down the steep slope to the level ground. Turning into the trail he rode at top speed, glancing upward at the walled bench from time to time. Where the ledge sluffed off against the cliff was a bulge. He rounded it and jerked Goldy to a dust plowing halt.

In the trail directly ahead lay three bodies. A quick glance identified them as the teamsters with whom he had talked the day before.

CHAPTER V

HATFIELD WASTED NO TIME examining the bodies. Face bleak, he rode on. He covered a mile and slackened speed. He knew he could easily overtake the slower traveling wagon. But the odds were too heavy to permit a direct attack on the owlhoots. He gauged his pace to hold the distance between him and the vehicle. The wide wheel marks in the dust were sufficient guide for the moment. The wagon could not turn off the trail without leaving evidence of the move.

For an hour he rode steadily, seeing nothing, hearing nothing. He reached the beginning of a long slope up which the trail writhed over broken ground. The crest stood out hard and clear against the sun drenched skyline. It still was a good five hours until sunset.

Hatfield negotiated the slope at reduced speed. Just below the crest he pulled up and dismounted. Leaving Goldy, he covered the remaining distance on foot. As he neared the lip of the sag, he left the trail and took advantage of all possible cover. Finally he reached a point where he could see over the crest.

The slope on the far side was even longer than the one he had just surmounted. The trail dropped steeply down it in a series of curves. And far ahead, approaching a bulge of cliff was the wagon and its escort. Hatfield counted four riders and two lead horses.

"The poor devils back there gave a good account of themselves," he muttered with satisfaction. "One jigger driving the team, and two bodies, or badly wounded men, tucked in the wagon. Five to one, as she now stands. Well, that isn't so bad. Now my chore is to keep out of sight till dark. Then we'll see how things size up."

He returned to his horse, mounted and rode boldly over the crest.

During the following hours, Hatfield twice spotted the wagon. He was confident that he himself had not been observed. Doubtless the robbers expected no pursuit and paid little attention to the terrain behind. When the shadows began crawling up the western slopes, Hatfield increased Goldy's pace until he had halved the distance between him and his quarry. As the blue dusk sifted down from the hilltops like an impalpable dust, he closed the distance between them even more. Finally he decided he was less than half a mile behind the wagon. Another hour, with dust having given way to darkness, and he felt that he had halved that. On the crest of a rise he pulled up and sat listening.

From the darkness below came a whisper of sound which he catalogued as the grind of wheels over the stones. Abruptly the sound ceased, which meant, he reasoned, that the owlhoots had either pulled off the trail or were preparing to make camp for the night.

After a moment of hesitation, he rode down the sag at a slow walk. He had covered but a few hundred yards when he again pulled the sorrel to a halt and sat quietly.

A short distance ahead he heard the clicking sound of horses' irons.

Hatfield's grip tightened on the bridle, preparatory to swerving the sorrel off the trail. But almost instantly he relaxed. The sound of hoofbeats faded away.

"Three or four horses," he muttered. "Now what?" Less than two hundred yards distance and a little to the left, a light shone in the darkness. It suddenly increased in intensity. A reddish flicker stained the crests of the brush ahead.

"Made camp for the night—lit a fire!" the Lone Wolf exulted. "And unless I'm mistaken, about three of the sidewinders rode on ahead for some reason or other. Maybe to tell the rest of the gang what had happened. Perhaps to decide how they are going to move the gold. They'll hardly risk taking the wagon much farther, and all that gold is too heavy to pack off on horseback. Chances are they sent for mules to handle it. This may work out all to the good."

He dismounted and led Goldy off the trail, concealing him in a clump of thicket. Then he regained the track and stole forward in the shadow of the growth.

The light of the fire grew stronger. Another moment and he could hear gruff voices conversing, and a rattle as of pots and pans being moved around. Doubtless the wagon contained cooking utensils and provisions.

With the utmost caution he stole on. Behind a final fringe of brush he paused and stared at the scene only a few yards distant.

The wagon had been drawn off the trail and stood beside a trickle of water seeping from under a huge boulder. Close by burned the fire. Two men moved about the blaze. Their horses and the wagon horses grazed on the bank of the little stream.

For some minutes, Hatfield watched and listened. Finally he decided that the two men beside the first were the only members of the outlaw band that remained with the wagon. The two riderless horses he had noted were also missing.

Swiftly he made his plans. He edged to the left of the camp, paused and drew his guns. His voice rang out—

"Elevate!"

The two owlhoots whirled, with startled exclamations. They stared unbelievingly at the tall figure walking slowly toward them. Then, screaming an oath, one went for his gun.

Hatfield shot him, dead center. He went down, kicking and

clawing. His companion scrambled to the side away from the fire. Hatfield shot, and missed. The owlhoot's gun blazed. A slug burned a red streak along Hatfield's cheek. The outlaw was in the shadow, his form an indistinct blur. A lance of flame split the shadows as he fired at the Ranger, who was racing toward him, weaving and ducking. The slug fanned Hatfield's face. Then both his Colts bucked and roared in his hands. He saw the shadowy form reel sideways, and fired again. The thud of the falling body came to his ears. He leaped beyond the ring of firelight and crouched.

But the sprawled form in the shadows did not move. Hatfield glided forward, guns ready. Then he lowered the Colts, ejected the spent shells and replaced them with fresh cartridges. The owlhoot was dead.

Standing in the darkness, Hatfield eyed the wagon. No sound came from the gloom under its top. He felt fairly convinced that it was unoccupied. But it would not do to be careless. A desperately wounded member of the band could be as danger-ous as a broken-back rattler. Finally he took a chance, plucked a brand from the fire and thrust it under the cover. Nobody was inside.

Throwing the torch aside, Hatfield returned to the dead men beside the fire. They were ornery looking specimens, typical border scum. With swift efficiency he examined the bodies. Looped around the neck of each was a handkerchief, flaming red in color.

The neckerchiefs were carefully folded to conceal eye-holes cut in them. A twitch upward and they would provide masks— the red masks of the notorious Scarlet Riders, or of imitators of the band.

"I'm beginning to get a notion these sidewinders are really members of the bunch, after all," he muttered as he went through the pockets of the dead men.

Of the odds and ends he discovered, only one thing interested him. It was a nickel badge with the legend, "Deputy Sheriff," cut in its surface.

"Wonder where he stole that?" the Ranger growled, pocketing the badge.

He investigated the wagon and found the sacks of gold pieces stored in a corner. From the number and weight of the sacks, he judged that none of the gold had been removed. Climbing out of the wagon, he studied the situation.

It was logical to believe that the three owlhoots he heard depart from the Gap would return. Doubtless they would bring others with them. To drive the wagon west along the trail would be to run the chance of encountering them. Hatfield had not the least desire to do that.

But no matter where he took the vehicle, the wheel marks would plainly reveal his course. To remove the gold and conceal it would take a long time. And time, he knew, was precious. He decided on a desperate expedient.

Working at top speed, he loaded the bodies of the dead owlhoots into the wagon. Their horses he tethered to the end-gate of the wagon. He harnessed the wagon horses and let them stand while he removed all evidence of the fight in the clearing. Then he climbed to the seat, turned the wagon into the trail and headed east.

As he passed the thicket where Goldy was concealed, he whistled. The sorrel came trotting onto the trail and took up a position behind the wagon.

"Now," Hatfield told himself, "everything depends on two things. First, that the farmers' wagon train made it through the Gap yesterday. Second, that I get to the trail forks south of the Gap before those sidewinders catch up with me. If the farmers passed there yesterday, the trail will be so cut up with wheel tracks that nobody will be able to tell whether this wagon passed that way. I'm playing a hunch that when the owlhoots get back to the clearing where the camp was made and don't find the wagon or the two jiggers they left to guard it, they'll figure their pals decided to do a little double-crossing and high-tailed it with the gold. Where would they go with it? To Dawes Landing and across to Mexico. At least that's what I hope they'll figure. Now if I can just make the trail forks in time!"

Getting the best possible speed out of the tired horses, he sent the wagon rolling eastward. On the crest of each rise, he glanced back over his shoulder. Each time the trail lay deserted in the moonlight with the marks of the broad tires clear upon it.

Dawn was streaking the sky when Hatfield reached the trail forks. He halted the team, leaped down and examined the surface of the Comanche Trail. To his infinite relief, it was cut and scored by a multitude of wheel tracks. The farmers had already passed through the Gap.

Hatfield turned the wagon into the Comanche and headed south. He drove for a short distance, carefully scanning the ground to the right of the trail. The strengthening light showed its stony and brush grown. Finally he reached a spot suitable for his purpose. He swerved the wagon from the trail and sent it lurching and bumping over the stony ground. Behind a thicket a hundred yards or so west of the trail, he pulled up. He slid down from the seat and retraced his steps to the trail.

Very little evidence of his leaving the trail was apparent. He broke a leafy branch from the chaparral and with the greatest care smoothed over the tracks left by the veering wagon. He replaced a few overturned boulders and made sure that no broken twigs hung down to the ground. Then he hurried to the wagon and urged the horses westward through the scattered growth.

The nearest hill slope was a quarter of a mile from the trail. Here, with the wagon concealed behind tall brush, Hatfield pulled up. He tied the team and mounted the slope until he had a clear view of the forks. He rolled a cigarette and settled himself comfortably to wait.

He did not wait long. Less than an hour passed before a group of speeding horesmen bulged into view from the west. Hatfield counted fourteen altogether. The distance was too great for him to distinguish features, but he noticed that a man riding slightly in advance of the others—evidently the leader—was broad-shouldered and tall.

The riders pulled up at the forks. The tall leader slid from his hull and paced back and forth across the Comanche. Hatfield saw him point to the ground. The others looked down from their saddles, and began talking exictedly.

Hatfield crouched low in the brush, every nerve strung to hair-trigger alertness. Another moment would decide his fate. His palms sweated at the thought that perhaps one of the hidden horses would begin to neigh. Such a sound would surely carry to the group on the trail.

The tall leader turned and looked up toward the high notch of the Gap which cut through the Santiagos. Then he turned to the west.

Hatfield's face grew tense. He tightened his grip on his rifle.

But suddenly the leader strode to his horse and mounted. He gave a command, and the troop headed south at a fast pace.

Hatfield relaxed with a sigh of relief. He chuckled as he watched the group stream over a distant rise and out of sight.

"Headed for the Landing," he told himself. "And I've a notion it'll take 'em a little time to make sure the wagon didn't go that way. Then, if my hunch is still straight, they'll hightail back to Persimmon Gap. They'll figure their pards turned north on the Comanche, aiming to make a get-away into the Pecos country. At least I hope they'll figure that way. If they don't, and decide to head west again, I may have an interesting time of it before I make Terlingua. Must be nigh onto fifty miles and the horses are tired. I'll turn 'em loose to graze for an hour and then light out."

CHAPTER VI

THE MOST AMAZED MAN in Texas was the manager of the Terlingua Mines when the treasure wagon pulled up in front of his office the following morning. The equipage was powdered with dust, the axles hot. The horses were on the verge of exhaustion. Hatfield's face was lined and haggard, his eyes red from lack of sleep. But he was in a decidedly complacent mood.

"What—how—why—" the manager stuttered.

Suppose you check the contents of those pokes first," Hatfield suggested. "Then we can talk. And I want the horses cared for. They need it."

"We'll put them in the company barn immediately," the manager replied. "I suppose that big sorrel is yours? Where are the riders of the other two?"

"You'll find 'em in the wagon, alongside the gold," Hatfield replied laconically. "Reckon they won't need horses any more."

The manager gulped and stared, but decided against asking further questions. Instead he began to bellow orders. He directed a clerk to guide Hatfield to the nearby company eating-house, set other employes to work packing the gold sacks into the office.

After a good bath and a satisfying meal, Hatfield returned to the mine office.

"Not a dollar missing," the manager said. "Now, tell me what happened. Where are the men we sent with the wagon? Who are those dead men and who killed them?"

In terse sentences, Hatfield told his story.

"No use trying to thank you for what you did," the manager said when Hatfield finished. "Words don't mean a thing at a time like this. I've a notion the directors will find a way to express their appreciation. You say the bodies of our men are down there on the Comanche Trail?"

"Unless the farmers picked them up and packed them along with them," Hatfield replied. "The chances are they did. They would have recognized them as the driver and guards of the wagon."

"I'll have the sheriff over at Marton notified right away," the manager promised.

"Sheriff's name is Snyder, isn't it?" Hatfield commented.

"Not any more," the manager replied. "Sheriff Snyder was defeated for re-election. A man named Fulton, Craig Fulton, got in last election. He owns a saloon in Marton, I believe. Seems to be all right, though. Hadn't held office a week before he recovered a stolen herd of cattle and killed two of the rustlers. I understand he routed a bunch of Mexican bandits too. I've a notion he may give the Scarlet Riders trouble before he's through with them. John Snyder was a good officer, but he was old. To my way of thinking, he spent too much time backing up Arch Wagner in his feud against the farmers. Wagner is the biggest ranch owner in the county."

Hatfield received this bit of news without comment. He recalled, however, that Captain McDowell had spoken favorably of Sheriff John Snyder.

"You say they're having a cowmen-granger row over there?" he asked.

"That's right," the manager replied. "And I understand it's getting worse. There's been considerable wire cutting and destruction of crops lately, and plenty of rustling. Wagner had a big barn burned and a waterhole poisoned."

Hatfield looked serious. This was an unexpected complication. The sort of a row that plays right into the hands of the owl-hoots, he told himself. Aloud he said, "Reckon I'd better ride to Marton and report to the sheriff. He'll want a first-hand account of what happened."

"Yes, that would be wise," the manager agreed. "I'll give you a letter to him. Do you figure to stay in this section for a while?"

"Maybe, if I can tie onto a job riding," Hatfield replied.

"No trouble about that," the manager said. "I'll give you a letter to Arch Wagner, too. Wagner is our biggest stockholder. He'll appreciate what you did. Saves him considerable money."

"Why did you have all that gold sent over here?" Hatfield asked.

"To meet payrolls and to pay for holdings to the south in which we're interested," the manager explained.

"Seems to me it would be safer to handle those transactions by check," Hatfield commented.

The manager shrugged. "No argument there," he replied, "but folks over here don't like paper. They want cash money—hard money. It means trouble and risk for us, but what can we do? The agreements drawn up by Judge Price, over at Marton, specify payment in cash."

Hatfield nodded. He understood the situation. Not even the big cattlemen liked paper. Buyers went well heeled with ready money, which all too often worked to the advantage of thieves and owlhoots.

"What I can't understand," said the manager, "is how those robbers learned the gold shipment was being made by boat."

"The presence of your mine wagon with the farmer's train was something of an advertisement," Hatfield suggested.

"I might agree with you, except that the wagon left here in the dead of night and didn't join the train until it reached the trail forks south of Persimmon Gap," replied the manager. "That point is less than a day's journey to Dawes Landing. Which would mean that the robbers had to see our wagon join the train there. That hardly seems reasonable. Why would the Scarlet Riders, if it was them, be down there?"

Hatfield nodded again. He recalled the cribbing built into the river, by which the level of the channel had been lowered. That chore took time.

"Yes, it begins to look like there was a leak somewhere," he admitted.

"It certainly does," the manager agreed emphatically. "I can't understand it."

Hatfield slept the clock around.

After another talk with the manager, he rode north by east in the shadow of the Christmas Mountains, Corazones Peaks, Red Bluff and the Nine Point Mesa. The bodies of the slain owlhoots had been dispatched to Marton the day before for inspection by the coroner and on the chance that somebody might identify them.

In his pocket Hatfield carried a letter addressed to Craig Fulton, sheriff of the county. A second letter introduced him to Arch Wagner, owner of the Open A spread.

With the sun low in the west, Hatfield rounded the northern tip of the Santiagos. On his left towered Elephant Mountain of the Del Nortes. Ahead was the pass between the two ranges, with Marton nearly twenty miles beyond. From a high bench he gazed eastward across the Toboso Flats, so named because of the prevalence of buffalo or toboso grass. In the dying sunlight the flats appeared to be a broad expanse of water.

The evening was peculiarly clear and bright. Far to the east, Hatfield could just make out the forms of ranchhouses and their outlying buildings. Tiny dots, he knew, were cattle feeding on the rich grass.

Directly below was something that interested him much more. Squares and rectangles of vivid green lay in the shadow of the mountain range. These were fields of crops. Farm buildings could also be distinguished.

The scene was peaceful, and beautiful. Hatfield shook his head.

"Seems that folks with such a nice country to live in could get along with each other," he told Goldy. "Doesn't make sense that they should waste time making trouble for one another. All right, feller, let's go. It'll be late before we make that darn town, and right now I'm ready for a surrounding of chuck. I can't fill up on grass like you did a ways back."

The trail, or what passed for one, wound down the long slope over a series of benches. Long before Hatfield reached the level ground below, night had fallen. Goldy was forced to pick his way carefully over the boulders and depressions. The moon shone down from a clear sky, but overhanging growth cast deceptive shadows across the track. Consequently, the going was very slow.

On the lip of a broad bench some five hundred feet above the level ground, Hatfield pulled Goldy to a halt. Below, the landscape was spread before his eyes like a map, softened and silvered in the moonlight. The slope the trail ran down jutted outward, a long tongue of broken land. To left and right the farm lands were clearly outlined. Beyond was level prairie. Hatfield could make out the moving blotches of cattle.

Suddenly he saw something else. Three horsemen were riding the trail from the east. As the Ranger watched them curiously, they branched off to the south, riding parallel to the wire that enclosed the farm lands. Within plain view of where Hatfield sat his horse they formed a huddle.

"Now what the devil are those hellions up to?" the Ranger wondered.

On the far side of the wire, but a few yards from it and directly in line with the horsemen was a tower-like structure some twenty or twenty-five feet in height. It looked like three stout ladders upright and spiked together, with a small platform on top. Hatfield had not the slightest notion what it was.

However, the three horsemen turned their attention to it. Suddenly they broke from their huddle, each one busily making preparations for some sort of action, but just what it was they planned to do Hatfield could not be certain.

"Darned if it doesn't look like they're building and twirling loops," he told Goldy. "What in blazes is there to rope down there? I can't see a thing."

A moment later he was sure one of the riders made a cast, although the rope was not apparent at that distance. Quickly the other two made similar motions, and it looked as if all three had tied onto something. The ponies backed up slowly, straining hard. Hatfield shook his head in bewilderment. Then he saw that the tall, tower-like structure was rocking and swaying.

"Damned if they aren't trying to pull that thing over!" he muttered. "Now what sort of a fool prank is this? They— thunderation!"

From the prairie below fluffed a blaze of reddish light and a cloud of smoke, through which Hatfield could see chunks of timber flying in every direction. The air rocked to the roar of an explosion.

Hatfield saw the horse nearest the tower jump into the air as if hit by a sledgehammer. The other two reared and danced then whirled and streaked across the prairie. Hatfield could hear their terrified snorts and the equally terrified yells of the riders.

The first horse rolled, kicked and scrambled to its feet. Its rider, staggering erect, made a frantic grab for the saddle horn. Running and leaping beside the fleeing cayuse, he managed to haul himself onto its back. A moment later he vanished from sight around a clump of thicket, the shadow of which had already swallowed his companions.

Hatfield whistled in amazement. As the smoke cloud dissipated, he saw a gigantic crater in the ground.

"Dynamite!" he exclaimed. "But how in blazes was it set off?"

His face was bleak as he regarded the ominous hole, black as pitch in the moonlight. The farmers undoubtedly had cause for resentment, but such retaliation, Hatfield thought, was carrying things a mite far. If the three riders had been close to the tower instead of being at the end of sixty-foot ropes, they would have been blown to bits.

Hatfield gathered up his reins and spoke to Goldy. The sorrel began picking his way down the trail. Before they were midway to the level ground, Hatfield saw lights to the south. Men on foot appeared, coming up along the line of the fence. They grouped around the gaping hole where the wooden structure had stood.

Without changing pace, Hatfield continued to ride down the trail. The men with the lanterns, he thought, were farmers attracted by the explosion. He knew they saw him coming and were puzzled, but he rode on nevertheless. He reached the level ground and turned Goldy's head toward the silent group. When he was within a score of yards of the farmers a voice ordered him to halt.

"That'll be about far enough, cowboy," said a grizzled, lanky man, stepping forward. "What's been goin' on here?"

Hatfield pulled Goldy to a halt.

"Reckon that's a question you can answer better than I can," he replied quietly.

The farmer moved nearer. He seemed puzzled at the Lone Wolf's remark.

"How's that?" he asked.

"Don't you figure it's a mite high-handed, planting dynamite that way?" Hatfield asked as the other, rifle in hand, paused a few feet from his stirrup.

The farmer stared at him. "What in tarnation are you talkin' about, anyhow?" he asked. His companions moved forward to join him.

Hatfield studied the old man with interest. The farmer's bewilderment seemed genuine enough.

"Did you see what happened here?" he asked. "Us fellers heard a big blow and come to see what more hell raisin' them dad-blamed ranchers were up to."

In a few words, Hatfield reported what he had witnessed.

The farmer tugged at his beard, and shook his gray head.

"Son," he said, "this is my land. I wouldn't plant any dynamite under that tower."

There was an undeniable ring of truth in the statement. Hatfield was well enough acquainted with the breed the old man represented to respect his sincerity.

"What was that thing for?" Hatfield asked, gesturing toward the ruin of the crazy-looking structure.

"A watchtower," the farmer explained. "A feller settin' up there could see over the prairie for miles and spot any ornery ranchers who were aimin' to meddle with our wire—it's been cut several times so as to let their cattle in to eat and tromp our crops. One moonlight night a couple of slugs came mighty close to the feller settin' up there, so we quit using it—too dangerous. You say somebody tried to pull it over?"

Hatfield nodded. "Three young punchers, likkered up and figuring to play a prank, I guess," he replied. "If they'd been closer to it they'd have stood a good chance of getting killed."

"Well, we didn't plant any dynamite there," the farmer declared.

"Somebody did," Hatfield put in. "Those three fellows were mighty lucky to be as far off as they were. I've a notion one of them got pretty badly shook up. Let's go over and see if we can learn how it was set off."

He dismounted and led the way to the crater.

"Bring the lanterns and go over the ground carefully," he called.

The farmers, without knowing just why, obeyed the order.

Hatfield already had a theory as to how the charge had been set off, and concentrated on the splintered supporting timbers. Examination of three of them proved nothing, but the fourth one interested Hatfield a great deal. A stout spike had been driven into one end of the support, leaving an inch or so of pointed metal exposed. The end of the timber was shredded and blackened, and the spike showed stains of powder smoke.

"Look at this," Hatfield said, holding a lantern close to the support. "The dynamite was planted at the base of this upright. The spike was set on the percussion cap. When the tower began to rock, the point of the spike struck the cap, and it doesn't take much to detonate a dynamite cap. When the cap exploded it set off the charge. See? Simple and devilish."

The farmers who had clustered around him stared in silence until one of them said in a suspicious voice—

"Feller, you seem to know a heap about it."

Hatfield smiled. Then he remarked in casual tones, "Did the folks from Del Rio arrive okay?"

Again there was silence, then another question, charged with more suspicion than the last—

"What do you know about them folks?"

"I rode across on the boat with them from Del Rio," Hatfield replied.

This time the silence was broken by the grizzled spokesman of the farmers.

"By gosh!" he exclaimed excitedly, "you must be the big feller they told us about, the feller who kept the engines goin' till they got off the burnin' boat! Be your name Hatfield?"

"Ever since I can remember," the Lone Wolf laughed.

The farmer stuck out a horny hand.

"Put 'er there, Hatfield!" he said. "I'm plumb pleased to meet up with you, and I reckon the rest of the boys are, too. My name's Brady, Moses Brady. Put 'er there!"

Hatfield shook hands all around, and acknowledged the names rattled off by Moses Brady.

"Where you headed for, son?" Brady asked.

"Marton," Hatfield told him.

"It's nigh onto fifteen miles, and it's late," Brady said. "I'd be proud if you'd spend the night at my place down the road. What do you say?"

"Reckon I couldn't do any better anywhere," Hatfield smiled.

"Fine!" Brady said. "There's a good helpin' of home-cooked vittles waitin', and a comfortable bed. But first we'll clear up this mess a bit and straighten them posts that are blowed loose."

While the farmers made repairs, Hatfield examined the smashed tower again. Noosed to a piece of timber he discovered about thirty feet of well-suppled manila rope.

"No wonder one of those jiggers turned a flipflop," he remarked to Brady. "He was tied hard and fast to that timber, and when his cayuse tried to romp off, the rope threw him before it broke. Wonder he didn't bust his neck."

He looped the broken rope and stowed it in his saddle pouch.

"Souvenir," he explained to Brady.

The farmers quickly repaired the fence.

"That'll hold 'em," said Brady, straightening his back. "I've a notion there won't be any more shindigs tonight, not after the racket that dynamite kicked up. Come on, son, let's go eat."

As they walked to Brady's farmhouse, which was about a quarter of a mile to the south, Hatfield asked a question—

"How come you fellers got here in such a hurry?"

"We were guardin' the wheat stands just to the south of here," Brady explained. "That's where those rapscallions can do some real damage, if they're smart. What we're scared of more than anything else at this time of the year is fire. Start a fire in the wheat and it would sweep the fields in no time. So far they haven't thought of that. Just cut the wire and let the stock in to eat the crops."

Hatfield nodded. "Funny thing," he remarked, "but it's hard to believe those jiggers would have attempted to tear down the tower if they'd known about that dynamite."

"It's beyond me," Brady replied. "I sure didn't plant that charge, and I'd be ready to swear none of our boys did."

Hatfield nodded again. "If you're right about those three fellers being cowhands from one of the spreads around here, there'd have been some trouble if they'd been blown to pieces."

Brady agreed solemnly.

"That's the kind of thing that starts a real range war," Hatfield continued. "Nobody's been killed hereabouts as yet, have they?"

"Not yet," Brady admitted, "but some of the boys workin' in the fields have been exposed to whistlin' lead."

Brady helped Hatfield put up his horse before they went into the small but well-built farmhouse.

Mrs. Brady, a motherly, gray-haired woman who was preparing supper, greeted Hatfield graciously.

"He reminds me of our Caleb," she said, smiling at her husband. Turning to Hatfield she added, "Caleb is our son who's studying to be a doctor back East." Then to her husband again, "Yes, Mose, he has the same look about the eyes and the same black hair."

"Uh-huh," agreed the farmer, "but he's bigger'n Caleb. Caleb is a six-footer, but this young feller is a heap taller than that."

As they sat smoking and waiting for the food to cook, Hatfield questioned the farmer about conditions in the section.

"This snappin' and snarlin' between the farmers and the cattlemen has been goin' on for a long time," Brady said. "We thought when we elected Bascomb Price a judge and Craig Fulton the sheriff, that things would be better. Instead, they're worse. Arch Wagner was mighty put out when his candidates lost the election. Reckon he thinks a mite better of Fulton now, but he still blames us fellers for his men losin'."

Hatfield sat in silence for a moment. "Suppose," he suggested at length, "that you start at the beginning and tell me how you fellers came to take up land here, and work up to the election upset."

"Okay," Brady agreed. "It's quite a story. I'll tell you all I know."

Mose Brady was a good talker, his explanations precise, almost picturesque at times.

Hatfield, eager to learn all that he could about the district, listened carefully.

Oldtimers said barbed wire would never come to the Big Bend country. But it did—with the arrival of the railroad.

Behind the new barricades grew broad acres of wheat, alfalfa and other crops. But the cultivated lands lay like a lamb encircled by the paws of a gigantic lion, a lion that was the rangeland extending to the horizon.

To Arch Wagner, the rust-red barbed strands were like thorns in his flesh.

Wagner was a grizzled cattle baron who, folks said, got his start running "wet" cows across the Rio Grande from Mexico. He owned the great Open A ranch with its large, luxuriously furnished casa, its deep, cool canyons and steadily flowing springs and its thousands of cows.

Self-satisfied to the point of arrogance, Wagner was the most powerful man in the district. His less fortunate neighbors deferred to him as an overlord, took to his advice, and obeyed his orders as a matter of course. Politically, he ruled the great county, which was as large as some eastern states. His backing helped put judges, commissioners, sheriffs and other officials into office. Men of his choosing went to the legislature and passed the laws Arch Wagner recommended. His influence extended to other counties as well. Candidates for governor sought his support when in quest of the nomination that was tantamount to election.

Wagner held sound title to his spread. His father had held it before him. The Wagner lands extended from the eastern county line to Terloga Creek. West of Terloga Creek was what Wagner had always considered open range. Though he used the grazing land west of the creek, he had never taken the trouble to gain title to it. Finally somebody else did. An eastern syndicate saw an opportunity for profit. After a careful investigation, the syndicate learned that the title was held by the Gomez family of Texas, rich, respected, of Mexican ancestry. The Gomez family held title by right of an ancient Spanish grant. The syndicate learned that the validity of the grant had been upheld by the Texas courts.

The Gomez family, as a matter of pride, had kept the taxes paid on the land, but otherwise took little interest in it. When approached by the syndicate and offered a fair price, they were only too glad to sell what they considered to be property of little value.

The syndicate proceeded to cash in on its investment. A number of farmers in east Texas were contacted and interested in the land. The syndicate strung wire, made certain improvements and helped move the farmers to the Big Bend country. Almost before Arch Wagner and his associates realized what had happened, the land west of Terloga Creek to the Presidio county line was occupied by grangers.

The syndicate moved on, but the farmers remained and prospered, despite constant feuds with Arch Wagner and his fellow-cattlemen.

This was the situation as election day drew near.

However, Wagner didn't worry about the outcome of the election. He had the votes, or thought he had. But whenever he thought of the opposition ticket headed by Bascomb Price, who was running for judge, he became enraged.

Bascomb Price was a lawyer of doubtful background. He had arrived in the section a few years earlier and hung out his shingle in Marton, the county seat. He had prospered. For whatever else might be said of Bascomb Price, he had ability. His knowledge of the law was exceeded only by his knowledge of how it could be evaded.

Price had helped the syndicate draw up its papers. He had won some cases for the farmers, others for small ranch owners. More than once he had opposed Arch Wagner. And more than once he had come out on top. He was shrewd, resourceful, fearless. He claimed to be a liberal. In fact, he was liberal with anything that did not immediately concern the welfare or prosperity of Bascomb Price. Where he himself was concerned, he was considerably more than conservative.

The farmers supported Price's candidacy. They were, to a man, behind anything that opposed Arch Wagner. But their voting power was not sufficient to swing an election. The cowmen and their hands, scattered about the sprawling countyside, commanded a comfortable numerical edge. Arch Wagner was not worried.

He would have been more concerned had he been able to follow Bascomb Price that summer and early fall as he rode about the county, pausing at small ranchhouses and chatting with their occupants.

For instance, if Wagner had overheard the conversation between Bascomb Price and Chet Johnson one warm and sunny day a few weeks before election, he would have been dismayed.

Chet Johnson was shiftless, and always in need of money, despite the fact that his spread could easily have been prosperous.

Several weeks before election Bascomb Price pulled up in front of Johnson's ramshackle ranchhouse and sat waiting, his long, lanky body lounging easily in the saddle. In a few minutes, Johnson appeared, and ambled down the broken steps to meet Price's big roan.

"Howdy, Bascomb," he said.

Price nodded, and looked expectantly at the ranch-owner. Johnson passed a nervous hand over his stubby chin.

"Bascomb," he said, "I'm scared I ain't quite ready to meet that note today, after all."

Price nodded, and asked an unexpected question—

"Figure to be in town on election day, Chet?"

Johnson looked surprised. "Why—why I ain't thought much about it," he replied. "Didn't figure there was much reason for takin' the trouble. Elections always go one way in this section."

"I thought maybe," Price said slowly, "that you and your hands might be in town on election day. Thought maybe your cousin Earl Jasper and his boys might be there, too."

Johnson rubbed his chin again, and appeared slightly perplexed, but thoughtful. He shot a questioning glance at Price, who was staring toward the blue hills in the west.

"Not in any particular hurry about the payment due on that note, Chet," Price said suddenly. "But I might be the day after election. Might be—*the day* after election."

Johnson stared at him again, but with new understanding in his eyes.

"Tell your cousin Earl hello for me when you see him, Chet," Price said, and rode on.

Johnson stared after him, rubbing his chin vigorously.

"By gosh, I've a notion I'd better ride over and see cousin Earl right now," he muttered aloud. "'*Might* be in a hurry the day after election!'"

Price's next stop was at the tight, well-kept ranchhouse of Calvin Rader. Rader didn't owe Price money. He didn't owe money to anybody. But, folks said, Calvin Rader would skin a flea to get the tallow. Bascomb Price had previously made it possible for Rader to make some profitable deals.

The conversation between Price and Rader was also brief.

"You and the boys figure to be in town on election day, Cal?" Price asked casually.

"Hell, no!" Rader growled reply. "Why should I waste a day's work to go there and vote for folks who'll be elected anyhow. Arch Wagner don't need our votes."

Price's hard blue eyes bored into Rader's filmy gray ones.

"Cal," he said, "if you and your boys happen to be in town on election day, I've a notion I might be able to introduce you to a buyer who'd take that herd you're getting together at a mite more than the average market price. In fact, I know I can, if you and your boys are in town that day."

Calvin Rader did not need a further explanation. His tight lips parted in what was meant to be a grin.

"I'll be there, Bascomb," he promised. "I'll bring the boys with me, and I'll pick up the Circle K bunch and bring 'em along, too. Kelton of the Circle K is sort of beholdin' to me, you know."

Bascomb Price visited other small spreads during the next few weeks. The conversations that ensued with their owners were similar to those with Johnson and Rader. They dealt with business matters, never with politics.

Price's final visit was to Val Carver, who owned the Cross C. Val Carver was an energetic young man with progressive ideas. He had bought the Cross C, an old, rundown spread, a few years before and had turned it into valuable property. Carver had had more than one run-in with Arch Wagner over methods of procedure. He had put Wagner in an angry mood by maintaining that the farmers would improve the section.

Carver was shrewd, industrious, and stubborn. And he was misguided enough to believe in the ticket that included Bas-

comb Price for judge and Craig Fulton, owner of the Queen
High saloon in Marton, for sheriff.

"Don't reckon we got much chance, Bascomb," Carver told
Price, "but I'll be there with my hands to cast a protest vote
against Wagner's shorthorn methods, anyhow."

"You might be surprised," Price predicted.

Carver smiled deprecatingly. " 'Fraid not," he replied. "All
the cowmen in the section swing in behind Wagner as a matter
of course, but maybe we can poll enough votes to give him a
jolt."

Mose Brady paused in his story to fill his pipe. "Carver got a
surprise, all right," he said to Hatfield. "And so did a lot of
other folks. I think that gives you a fair idea of how Price
swung it even though I haven't told you all the details."

There were indeed certain "details" of the political scheme
with which Mose Brady was not familiar. If he had been, and
had been able to pass them on to Hatfield, subsequent happenings might have turned out differently.

The night before election, Bascomb Price had a visitor who
slipped quietly into his darkened office, glided across the room
and knocked on an inner door.

A bolt sounded and the door opened a crack, revealing a
closely shuttered room lighted by a hanging lamp.

"Come in," said Price. He quickly closed the door after the
other, and bolted it. They sat down on opposite sides of a table
under the hanging lamp.

The visitor was a tall, powerfully built man of thirty or a
little more. He had a smooth, deeply tanned complexion, eyes
that were such a dark blue that they appeared black in the lamp-
light, a tight-lipped mouth and a long, powerful chin. For a
long moment he regarded Price steadily.

"Well?" he said at length.

"Well," replied the lawyer, "I've done everything I could,

and I figure we've nothing to worry about. I've a notion Arch Wagner is in for a surprise, tomorrow."

"You saw everybody, as I told you to?"

"That's right. Spent a little money where I 'lowed it would do the most good. Never told anybody, directly, to come to town and vote our ticket. Call any one of 'em before a grand jury and they couldn't testify a thing to that effect."

"If there's any grand jury prying into your affairs, it will be about something other than vote buyin'," the stranger grunted.

Price's teeth showed in what was almost a snarl.

"There's no need to talk that way," he growled.

The other's lips twitched. His eyes seemed to darken.

"I hope I won't have to," he replied in amused tones.

Bascomb Price disregarded the last remark.

"You know," he said, "I've a notion I'm goin' to begin a real political career tomorrow."

"Reckon not," the other said dryly, "not with what you got hangin' over your head."

The lawyer's face darkened.

"Who the hell would dig that up?" he demanded.

"Don't know," the other replied, "but *somebody* might, if things get out of hand."

"Don't threaten me," Price snapped.

"I'm not threatenin'; I'm just tellin' you how things stand," the other replied quietly. "You know it as well as I do. No cause for any high-falutin' notions about goin' respectable. You couldn't do it, Price. You just ain't made that way. You'd rather make one crooked dollar than five honest ones. Besides, you sort of owe me and the boys something. If it wasn't for me, you'd be—somewhere else."

Bascomb Price looked like a cornered rat, but a very dangerous rat. He glared at his companion. But when he spoke, his voice held nothing of rancor, only protest.

"The trouble with you, Kenton, is that you can't see a foot

beyond your nose," he said. "You can always see the pesos that are close at hand, but you can't see the thousands a mite farther on, the thousands we could have if you'd string along with me."

Kenton nodded, gazing steadily at the lawyer. "I admit you got a point there, Price," he said. "But I can't see it any different. The only way we can win is to make a good profit as quickly as possible and then trail our twine. How would you stand the advertisin' that a political career would bring you? You're smart. I'll admit that. But are you smart enough to figure that one out?"

"There's a way, and I've a notion I can figure it out," Price replied slowly.

"Okay," Kenton agreed instantly. "You figure it. But a thing like that takes dinero and we ain't got it. And the boys will have to be took care of. They ain't goin' to sit around with empty pockets, twiddlin' their thumbs, and you know it."

"They'll be taken care of," Price assured him. "But we've got to play it smart. I've got some ideas I'll put into effect as soon as we get control of things. One of them is to win Arch Wagner and his bunch over to our side. I can do it."

"Do that, and we'll be settin' pretty," nodded Kenton. "The feller I'm scared of more'n anybody else is that young feller, Val Carver. He's got brains, and if things don't work out the way he figures they should, he's liable to make trouble."

"He'll be taken care of," Price promised grimly.

The other nodded, and rose to his feet.

"I'll be amblin'," he said, "want to be back to the hills before daylight. Got a mite of business to attend to. Reckon everybody else, includin' the sheriff, will be busy with the election tomorrow."

Price seemed to understand. "We'll need that money," he said. "Be sure you get it."

"I'll get it, all right," the other promised as he took his departure.

Arch Wagner was in town early the following morning. The election results would depend on the ballots cast in Marton. The scattered vote over the rest of the county being negligible.

Wagner was in a complacent frame of mind. To his way of thinking, the election was fixed. He was not disturbed when the farmers began to arrive. Their vote would be cast solidly against his ticket. That was a foregone conclusion. But they were not strong enough numerically to change the result. The big spread owners and their hands, who could be counted on to vote in accordance with their employers' wishes, outnumbered the farmers. This election, like those preceding it for many years, would be but a ratification of royal edict from the barons of the range.

But my mid-afternoon, Wagner's complacency and peace of mind were things of the past. Aghast, astounded, he watched the unprecedented number of ballots cast. By horseback, buggy, wagon and buckboard, they came—men who had not exercised their right of franchise for years. And Wagner knew very well they had not come to town to vote for the candidates he, Wagner, sponsored.

"Somebody's talked them fellers into comin' to town and vote," Wagner declared to old Judge Bennet, who had held his office for a decade or more.

"One guess," Bennet replied grimly.

"That goddam Bascomb Price, that's who," raged Wagner.

"Arch," the judge said slowly, "I reckon you needn't blame Price over-much. The fellers really to blame are you and me and the rest of the boys. We never paid those little fellers any mind. Never went to the trouble to bring 'em in with us against the time when we'd need 'em. Oh, I know, we didn't used to need 'em. And we never did anything for 'em to make 'em line up with us. We just let 'em slide. We had all the votes we needed without 'em. But now it's a different story. With the farmers, they got enough votes to turn us fellers upside-down, and I've a notion that's just what they're goin' to do."

Judge Bennet had a straight notion. Long before the last ballot was counted, the Price ticket had won hands-down.

The farmers, and Val Carver, proceeded to go wild. But they could not look into the future to see what their jubilation would mean.

With the election results officially confirmed, Craig Fulton, owner of the Queen High saloon in Marton, took over the sheriff's office. He immediately appointed as deputies one of his bartenders, a former cowhand, and his head dealer, to the infinite disgust of Arch Wagner and his associates.

"Decent folks might as well move out of the section right now!" stormed Wagner.

He was in an even stormier mood when he tore into town the following week and shook his fist under Sheriff Fulton's nose.

"Started already, eh?" he bellowed.

"What's started?" asked the sheriff. "What's the matter?"

"What's the matter?" mimicked Wagner. "A hundred prime beefs stole from my west pasture, and one of my hands with a bullet-busted shoulder! That's what's the matter!"

The sheriff remained calm.

"When did it happen?" he wanted to know.

"Happened this mornin', in broad daylight," rumbled Wagner. "The sidewinders don't even take the trouble to wait till it's dark any more. They know they ain't got nothin' to worry about."

"Which way did they go?" Fulton asked quietly.

"Which way would they go but west into the hills?" snorted Wagner. "My boys are hightailin' after 'em, but they got a good start and they know the country, of course. My beefs are gone."

"Reckon they took the Terlingua Trail, which would mean they'd circle south," mused the sheriff.

Within ten minutes, Sheriff Fulton and his two deputies rode out of town, headed west by south. Wagner watched them go, with sneers and profanity.

There was a different expression on his bad-tempered old face two days later, however, when Sheriff Fulton and his deputies returned. Ahead of them trudged a herd of weary, disgusted cattle. Behind, trudged two horses bearing meaningless Mexican brands. Roped to the saddle of each horse was a dead man.

"There were two or three more of the sidewinders," explained the sheriff, "but they give us the slip. But we got the cows and brung along them two back there as souvenirs."

"A good chore," Wagner admitted grudgingly.

Sheriff Fulton nodded. "Wagner, I know you ain't got no use for me," he said, "I know you figure I ain't worth a damn. But maybe I'll do a better chore than you figure. I got a lot to learn, but I aim to do my duty as I see it. Nobody is goin' to raise hell in this county and get by with it, so long as I can help it."

Wagner was still not thoroughly convinced. He couldn't resist another sneer—

"Suppose you'll be bringin' in the Scarlet Riders next!"

"That," the sheriff admitted frankly, "is considerable of a chore. "It's a plumb salty bunch with somebody runnin' it who's got plenty of savvy. They know every crack and gully over to the west, which is more than I do. They 'pear to always know what's goin' on. Sheriff Snyder wasn't no snide, but he didn't have much luck against 'em. I'll do my best, Wagner, and that's all anybody can do. Why can't you give me credit for that, even though you and me don't always see eye-to-eye on everything?"

After arranging for the care of his recovered herd, Arch Wagner went off in a thoughtful mood.

Young Val Carver of the Cross C was exultant.

"Knew we was backin' the right horse," he told the gathering of farmers. "Fulton won't stand for no nonsense from anybody, and Judge Price will back him to the limit. I figure we're in for better times hereabouts."

Bascomb Price heard of what Carver said, and grinned.

There was an unfortunate gap in Mose Brady's story. Brady would have been considerably startled had he overhead the conversation when Webb Kenton again visited Bascomb Price in his office.

"See you put it over, all right," Price chuckled. "Wagner is plumb pleased about getting his cows back, and he's beginning to feel uncertain about Fulton."

"Nothin' to it," returned the tall Kenton. "The boys grabbed off the herd easy. That fool cowhand showed up while they were runnin' 'em off Wagner's range and they had to plug him. They thought he was done for, but he evidently come to after they rode off. Lucky he didn't get his senses back too soon or we might have had trouble. Wagner has got some cold propositions ridin' for him and if they had caught up with the boys before they got in the clear, there would have been trouble."

"That cowhand didn't get a good look at any of the boys?" Price asked rather anxiously.

"Nope. They took care of that. Remember, it was daylight. The boys had handkerchiefs—*black* handkerchiefs—tied over their faces."

"Where did Fulton come up with you?"

"We were waitin' down in the south pass. Had the cows holed up in a canyon. We shoved 'em out and started him back to town with 'em."

Bascomb Price nodded. Suddenly a thought seemed to strike him.

"Who were the two fellers Fulton packed into town with him?" he asked.

Kenton shrugged his broad shoulders. "I don't know," he replied. "They were a couple of chuck line ridin' cowhands what come along while we were helpin' Fulton get started. Said they were headin' for New Mexico."

"They suspected something?"

"Nope. Why should they?"

"Then why did you have to cash them in?"

"Didn't have to," Kenton replied, his thin lips stretching in a wolfish grin. "I just figured it would make Fulton's hand look stronger if he brought a couple of bodies along with the cows."

Price stared at the other, met his darkly blue, glowing eyes regarding him speculatively, and shuddered.

"Kenton, sometimes I wonder if you aren't the Devil himself," he said slowly.

The other grinned again.

"No sense in doin' things halfway," he replied composedly.

"You never do," Price agreed with emphasis. "You always go the whole way. But I wish you hadn't had to down that blasted Ranger on the train that day," he worried.

"Didn't know he was a Ranger," Kenton replied. "Not that it would have made any difference. He was reachin', and I had to let him have it. I'm beginning to think the Rangers are a mite over-rated. That one showed plenty of guts, but he sure didn't show no judgment. And guts ain't enough to get you by."

"There are Rangers who've got guts and judgment, too," Price said grimly. "I haven't felt right since that happened. I've been expecting McDowell to send a troop over here because of it. And we don't want a bunch of those devils snooping around. Things are hot on the Border farther east just now, though, and McDowell is pretty busy. Besides, I learned that young feller you killed had been with the Rangers only a few months. Perhaps he was hardly considered one of them yet."

"Me and the boys will take care of any Rangers that happen along," Kenton replied complacently. "You just handle your end here and I'll take care of mine. Did you get the lowdown on that gold shipment coming up the Rio Grande? Yeah? Good!

Let's have the line-up. Ninety thousand dollars! Whe-e-ew! And you're sure it's going to be handled that way? Well, reckon there is something to being a judge and a political boss. Okay, we'll start in the morning. Got several days ride ahead of us, and work to do when we get to Dawes Landing. Don't worry about me handling it. I know every inch of that section down there and I got my plans made. Somebody is sure in for a surprise."

Hatfield suddenly realized that Brady had fallen silent and was regarding him with a twinkle in his faded eyes.

"Mose, you're a wonderful talker," he complimented the farmer. "You sure made it all sound real."

"Yep, as I said before, an interesting yarn," Brady replied. "I've a notion there's considerable more to it that I ain't heard about. The way it worked out sure riled Arch Wagner considerable."

"Wagner is a sort of big skookum he-wolf in this section, eh?" Hatfield remarked.

"Uh-huh. He ran things for so long he got the notion anything he did was right, I reckon," Brady replied. "I've a notion he ain't such a bad feller, down to the bottom, but he's sure uppity. All the other big ranchers foller his lead, too. That is except young Val Carver who owns the Cross C ranch, and Webb Kenton of the Open Diamond O. Carver has always been friendly with us fellers. He sells us meat, and he's bucked Wagner more than once over the way he carries on. They had a pretty serious row just last week. Got into an argument in town. Wagner knocked Carver down—Wagner's a big, husky feller. Carver reached for his gun, but Wagner shot first and knocked a hunk of meat out of Carver's arm. Judge Price bound 'em both over to keep the peace, but I've a notion it ain't finished yet."

Hatfield nodded, his eyes serious. Undoubtedly real trouble was building up in the section. For the moment he forgot all about the Scarlet Riders and their depredations. His experience was that an owlhoot bunch was easier to deal with than a range war.

"What about the other feller, Kenton?" he asked.

"Oh, Kenton is all right," Brady replied. "He's a funny feller in some ways. 'Tends strictly to his own business. Says he's got enough trouble makin' a livin' without mixin' in other folks' rows. He's friendly enough to us fellers, and he gets along with the other cattlemen, too. Even with Arch Wagner, though I figure Wagner holds a mite of a a grudge against him."

"How's that?" Hatfield asked as he rolled a cigarette with the slim fingers of his left hand.

The farmer chuckled. "Kenton plumb outsmarted Wagner in a deal," he explained. "It was like this: Webb Kenton showed up in this section a couple of years back. Appeared to have considerable money and nothin' much to do. He rode around, lookin' the country over, makin' friends with folks and learnin' about the cattle business here. One day he rode to Arch Wagner's place and made him an offer for his holdin's down to the south of here. Wagner jumped at the chance to sell, and figured he'd sure put over a smart deal."

Brady chuckled, and stuffed tobacco into his pipe. He blew out a cloud of smoke, and resumed—

"But it was Kenton who was plumb smart. This is a funny country, this southwest Texas country. Everything is topsyturvy. Over to the east of here is Terloga Crik—just the other side that line of trees you can see from the front door. Up to the north a ways, Terloga Crik runs over our land, that we haven't fenced and don't use yet. It's a big crik and never goes dry. It gives us plenty of water for our irrigation. Just above where you rode down the trail, the crik turns east a mite and runs on south over Arch Wagner's land. Wagner's land is good land with springs and waterholes on it and another crik over farther to the east. But ten miles to the south, below our holdin's is a high ridge that runs across this valley from east to west. When Terloga Crik butts up against that ridge, it turns west and follows the ridge toward the hills over to the west. Before it hits the hills, it scoots into a cave under a cliff and never shows up again, so far as anybody knows. That is, it never *used* to show up."

Brady paused to light his pipe again. Hatfield maintained an interested silence. He began to divine what was coming.

"Well," resumed Brady, "down south of that big ridge is the land Wagner sold Kenton. It's nice, level land with good grass growin' on it, and thickets and trees. But it didn't have a drop of water on it for cattle to drink. Wagner never run any cows down there, and because the land seemed plumb worthless for cattle raisin', of course he was glad to sell."

"And figured Kenton for a plumb sucker," Hatfield interpolated.

"That's right," Brady nodded. "But Kenton sure wasn't no sucker. Down south of the ridge, the base of the west hills is a long line of cliffs, big tall ones. Well, Kenton noticed something down there that everybody else had overlooked. The cliffs were all growed over with ferns and lichens and such truck. Kenton went to the cliff where the ferns was growin' thickest. He planted some big dynamite charges and set 'em off."

Brady paused again, his faded blue eyes twinkling.

"Go on," Hatfield urged.

"The dynamite blew a big hole in the cliff," Brady continued his story. "And I'll be gosh-darned if a great big stream of water didn't come tumblin' out of that hole. What do you know about that!"

"Terloga Creek running underground, of course," Hatfield said. "That's not uncommon in this region. The Big Bend country, and over east for a long ways, has one of the most intensive underground water systems in the world. As the Rocky Mountain chain rose, millions of years ago, bringing the mountains of western Texas with it, the crust of the earth was tremendously faulted. The fault zone in Texas is easily identifiable from Del Rio to San Antonio, for example. Ground water made caverns and stored supplies for future artesian wells, and so on. Ground water came from the faulting and originated rivers like the San Antonio, the San Marcos and the Guadalupe. In the long run the underground water supplies will prove to be among Texas' most valued resources. It will eventually make garden spots out of what is now desert land. As you fellers doubtless know, the enormous flow from the springs around Del Rio is responsible for the agricultural prosperity over there."

"Son, you talk like a college feller, or like Webb Kenton when he gets goin' good," old Brady said admiringly. "I don't understand much what you're sayin', but I reckon it's right. Anyhow, Kenton sure got plenty of water. He directed the flow, dug ditches and waterholes and sort of turned what you might call desert land into one of them garden spots, I reckon. He brought in cattle—good ones. He's been bringin' in more of late, and I reckon he's doin' pretty well.

"A feller like him usually does," Hatfield agreed. "And you say Wagner didn't like it?"

"Oh, I reckon it wasn't unnatural for him not to like it over well," Brady replied. "He never said much and he stayed friendly to Kenton, on the outside, anyhow, but I've heard he kicks himself around his barn every time he thinks about it."

Hatfield chuckled, and sat down to table at Mrs. Brady's call.

CHAPTER VII

WHILE HATFIELD SLEPT PEACEFULLY under Moses Brady's hospitable roof, there was a wrathful meeting in Bascomb Price's law office in Marton. Webb Kenton was there, his blue eyes so dark with anger that they looked black. There also was Sheriff Craig Fulton and Deputy Chuck Davis, the former bartender.

"It was the worst bungled job I ever heard of," Price declared furiously. "Ninety thousand dollars as good as ours, and we lose it. Kenton, why do you always think you know better than anybody else? Why do you always insist on doing things the hard and complicated way just to show how smart you are? Right from the beginning I didn't favor that attack on the steamer. If you'd laid low, like I advised, and swooped down on the wagon, everything would have been okay. But no! You had to figure out a fool plan with fancy angles, botch it and give the whole thing away."

"That try for the steamer was all to the good except for one thing," Kenton defended himself. "I figured things out just right, laid my plans accordingly and wrecked the boat. But how was I to know they'd have a chain-lightnin' two-gun man on that infernal boat? If it hadn't been for him we wouldn't have had any trouble. The farmers weren't armed, and we would have handled the crew easy. That jigger, whoever he was, threw the boys plumb off balance. Then the boat slewed out into the middle of the river and down it went, in flames. There was nothing we could do then. From all indications, that gold was headed for the bottom of the Rio Grande. I was already figuring a way to get it up again. But somehow they got the boat to the shore and unloaded it. I kept close tabs on them, saw the wagon leave the Landing after dark and shot on ahead with the boys. Everything worked out perfect."

"Except for half a dozen good men dying," Price growled. "The one smart thing you did, Kenton, was to pack those two bodies off with you when you went to fetch the mules. Suppose they had arrived here with those other two? That would have started something that would have meant the finish for all of us."

"What I want to know," growled Sheriff Fulton, "is who is that damned cowhand who did for the boys and grabbed the wagon?"

"And what I want to know is how did he do it?" stormed Kenton. "I'm still up in the air about that!"

"The note from the mines manager didn't say," replied Fulton. "I reckon maybe we'll learn when he shows up here. That is, if he shows up. He may decide it's the healthy thing for him to trail his rope out of this section."

"It's goin' to be unhealthy for him, all right," Kenton declared vindictively. "I'm out to even the score with him, personally. What are you goin' to do if he shows up, Fulton?"

"What the hell can I do but shake hands with him and tell him what a fine chore he did?" snorted the sheriff. "Sometimes, Webb, you talk like a plumb damn fool!"

"That'll be about enough of that from you!" Kenton replied, his eyes narrowing to slits.

"Here! here! Stop it!" Price interrupted. "We've got enough on our hands without starting a ruckus among ourselves. I tell you, I'm worried. That fellow doesn't sound like any ordinary chuckline-riding cowhand to me. Did anybody get a look at him?"

"I sort of glimpsed him from the riverbank," Kenton replied. "He looked about seven feet tall and broad as a barn door. But the light wasn't over good, and after he put a rifle slug through my hat I moved back a mite."

Price looked as if he sort of wished the slug had been a little lower, but he refrained from putting his thoughts into words.

"Well," he said, "he should show up here tomorrow, if he shows up at all. I think everybody should be hanging around for a look at him."

"I'll be here," Kenton promised grimly.

"And you'd better appoint another deputy, Fulton," Price added. "By the way, what are you giving out about Bob Raines?"

"Oh, Raines *resigned* three days ago and left for southern Arizona," Fulton replied. "I'm passing the word around."

"Southern Arizona *is* sort of hot," Price remarked dryly.

The remark, which was apparently intended to be humorous, was not well received by his hearers, who glowered instead of smiling.

After a hearty breakfast, Hatfield said good-bye to the farmer and his wife and headed for town. As he rode across the rolling rangeland, he was more and more impressed by the evident prosperity of the section. The cows were fat and numerous, the buildings he saw were all in good repair. He noted nearly a dozen different brands in the course of his ride. Most numerous were the Open A's. Evidently Arch Wagner was a man bountifully endowed with this world's goods. Hatfield wondered just what sort of a person he was. He did not judge Wagner from his attitude of intolerance toward the farmers and barbed wire. That attitude had been built up in the course of the years, and was shared, he well knew, by nearly all the oldtime cowmen.

He knew, too, that such men as Wagner would be forced to change their attitude. Barbed wire had come to the west to stay.

It would be but a matter of time until the ranchers themselves would realize its value and adopt it.

In fact, this had already happened in many parts of Texas. In the Panhandle section there were thousands of miles of wire strung, and more being strung all the time. The Big Bend country was one of the last strongholds of the open range. But, Hatfield clearly foresaw, the open range was fast going the way of the bony, angular longhorn. He smiled as he passed the grazing examples of improved stock. The cows feeding on Arch Wagner's range were heavy with succulent beef and showed the results of careful breeding.

"Yes, wire and the farmers are here to stay," he told Goldy. "And the quicker fellers like Wagner admit the fact, the better off they'll be. Nobody can turn back the wheels of progress."

But he knew that the situation as it stood at present promised trouble and bloodshed. It had happened before. He felt that his primary chore was to prevent such happenings here.

"Somebody is out to make trouble," he declared with conviction. "Old Moses Brady wasn't lying when he said he didn't plant that dynamite. Whoever did it was deliberately trying to foment trouble. What I'd like to know more than anything else is how did those three fellers get the notion to overturn that abandoned tower?"

He reached into his saddle pouch and fingered the section of broken rope stowed there.

"This bit of busted twine," he mused, "may give me the answer. I'm playing a hunch with it; here's hoping it turns out to be a straight one."

It was nearly noon when Hatfield reached his destination. Marton proved to be a typical border country cow town. Board sidewalks, long lines of hitchracks, false fronts, lanterns hung on poles at the corners to provide illumination. Every other building, it seemed, housed a saloon, dance hall, gambling joint or eating house. The crooked main street was deep in dust. There was a bustle of business in the general stores. A babble of conversation drifted through the open windows and over the swinging doors of the saloons.

Hatfield rode slowly through the outskirts. He assumed that, as was usual in county seats, the sheriff's office and the calaboose would both be housed in the building that served as a courthouse and would be on the main street near the business section.

His surmise proved correct. He hitched Goldy at a convenient rack, crossed the street to the squat building and located a door over which was a battered wooden sign lettered "Sheriff's Office."

The door stood partly open. Hatfield entered without knocking. As he strode into the room, two men looked up from a desk at which they were sitting.

One was a florid, bulky individual with fat jowls, a rather loose mouth and squinty eyes set in rolls of flesh. On his sagging vest was pinned a large silver shield that proclaimed him sheriff of the county.

His companion was a totally different breed. Lean, lanky with a rat-trap visage, his mouth tight, his deeply-set blue eyes very keen. Altogether he had the look of an able and adroit man. His hands, long, blue-veined, with supple, tapering fingers, rested on the desk before him.

Hatfield, who missed nothing, saw those hands abruptly grip the edge of the desk till the knuckles whitened.

The man's face, however, remained impassive, wearing only a look of polite inquiry.

"Howdy?" greeted the sheriff. "Something I can do for you?"

"I have a letter for you, suh," Hatfield said, drawing the missive from his pocket. "It's from Austin, the manager of the Terlingua Mines."

The sheriff took the letter, opened it casually and glanced at the contents. Then he leaped to his feet, grabbed Hatfield's hand with what was apparently intended for great heartiness and pump-handled it vigorously.

"Feller," he exclaimed, "I've already heard about you, and I'm plumb glad to meet you. Want to congratulate you on the plumb good chore you did. And here's somebody else who'll be glad to see you. I want you to know Judge Bascomb Price. The Terlingua Company was one of the judge's clients before he got elected to office and retired from private practice for a spell. Judge, this is Jim Hatfield—the one they told us about when they brought in the bodies of those two owlhoots day before yesterday."

Bascomb Price rose to his feet and shook hands with a firm grip.

"This is a pleasure, Hatfield," he said in a deep and resonant voice. "Sit down and tell us about it."

Hatfield accepted the invitation. In a few quiet sentences he recounted the happenings on the trail. The sheriff clucked in his throat. Bascomb Price nodded pontifically.

"Almighty smart work," he chuckled. "Those miscreants must have been mighty bold. Wait till they hear about what really happened. There'll be some fancy swearing over in the hills or I'm a lot mistaken.

"But, Hatfield," he continued in graver tones, "you've made some bad enemies. That bunch has given us a world of trouble in the past year. The sheriff is on their trail, but so far they've outsmarted even him."

"They know every hole and crack in the hills," growled Sheriff Fulton. "Twice I've thought I had 'em cornered, but each time they've dodged the loop. I'll get 'em yet, though, damn 'em!"

He frowned ferociously as he spoke. Bascomb Price nodded agreement.

"It's just about time to eat," he remarked. "Suppose we go over to Queen High and put away a helpin'. Sheriff Fulton owns the Queen High and we'll get good service. This afternoon the coroner will want to hold an inquest over those bodies. We waited till you got here, Hatfield. A lot of folks will be in town for the inquest. Want you to meet them."

The inquest was held a couple of hours later. It was short. The verdict was also short, and to the point. It congratulated Hatfield on having done a good chore and advised that the sheriff hustle up and polish off the rest of the sidewinders.

After the formalities were over, a number of cowmen came up to Hatfield to add their commendations to those of the coroner's jury.

Foremost was a big, beefy, powerful-looking man with snapping black eyes and an arrogant expression. His mouth, Hatfield noticed, was finely formed and grin-quirked at the corners. The Lone Wolf was not at all surprised when he introduced himself as Arch Wagner. He shook hands with great heartiness.

"Mighty glad to know you, son," he boomed. "Hope you'll see fit to stick around a spell. This section needs folks like you."

Hatfield smiled down at the old cattle baron, liking him at once, and understanding him.

"Reckon that sort of depends on you, suh," he said, passing the mine manager's letter to Wagner.

Arch Wagner read the letter, a pleased expression on his lined, bad-tempered old face. He shook hands again.

"Austin says you're lookin' for a job," he said. "Well, you don't have to look any more, if you care to tie on with me. I'd want you anyhow, but right now I'm glad to get a few extra hands. Gettin' a whoppin' big herd together and a long and hard drive ahead of me. Sellin' the critters to the Dawes outfit down by the river. They're expandin' their holdin's—it's an eastern combine, you know—and want stock. You'll get to see the Landing again, if you sign up. Reckon you could do without that, though, after what you went through down there."

"Was interesting, anyhow," Hatfield smiled reply. "I'll be plumb glad to sign with you, suh."

"Fine! Fine!" Wagner applauded. "Now I want you to meet

some of the boys. This here is Webb Kenton, who plumb out-smarted me in a deal but is all right just the same. Kenton, shake hands with Jim Hatfield. You know all about him already. Saw you in the courthouse."

Webb Kenton's hand was like a steel vise. His darkly blue eyes rose a little to meet Hatfield's level green eyes, but very little. Hatfield reckoned Kenton within a couple of inches of his own height. Kenton's dark features were cameo-perfect, his mouth tight-lipped, his jaw long and powerful.

"Glad to know you, Hatfield," he acknowledged Wagner's introduction. "Hope you'll stay with us a long time, and I've a notion you will."

"Never can tell," the Lone Wolf agreed. " 'Pears to be a nice section with interesting folks in it."

"Would be nice if it wasn't for them damned nesters over to the west," growled Wagner, his heavy face flushing. "And them what stands in with 'em," he added.

Kenton smiled, showing sharply pointed teeth of a singular whiteness, but did not comment.

"Be seeing you, folks," he said, and strode away, walking with lithe grace and very lightly for so large a man.

Sheriff Fulton strolled up at that moment. Wagner greeted him with a nod.

"Who you aim to appoint as deputy, now that Raines has left you?" he asked.

"Haven't decided yet," the sheriff replied. "I'll get somebody."

"Raines go back to dealin' cards?" Wagner asked.

"So he said," Fulton answered. "Said it was an easier way to make a livin' than dodgin' lead. I offered him his old job back in my place, but he said he felt like movin' around a bit. Wanted to look the country over."

"Never saw a gambler who could stay put in one place for long," Wagner declared. "They either move on or get moved."

"Oh, Bob won't ever have any trouble; he's a straight dealer," the sheriff said.

"Always heard he was," Wagner admitted. "Well, be seein' you. Let's have a drink, Hatfield, and then, if you're agreeable, we'll ride down to my place. Reckon you passed it on your way here."

Hatfield nodded, recalling the big comfortable-looking ranchhouse advantageously placed on a rise that overlooked the trail to Marton. He had felt sure as he rode past that it was the *casa* of Arch Wagner.

"A mighty fine-looking place," he commented as they moved across the street together.

"Uh-huh, my dad built it," said Wagner. "About the best in the section, I reckon. The old man wasn't the sort to stint."

As they walked to the bar in the Queen High, Wagner's big form suddenly stiffened, his face flushed darkly. Following the direction of his hot gaze, Hatfield saw a slender, well-formed young man standing near the far end of the bar. He carried his right arm in a sling.

Wagner saw that Hatfield had noticed his irritation.

"That's Val Carver down there," he said, jerking his head toward the quiet drinker. "You'll hear about him sooner or later. He sides with the nesters and has caused me plenty of trouble. I busted him one the other day."

Hatfield glanced at his companion. "Considerable under your weight, wouldn't you say?" he remarked.

Hatfield spoke smilingly, but Wagner understood the implied reproof. He glared at his new hand.

But Hatfield's steady green eyes did not waver as they met Wagner's resentful look. And something in their level gaze appeared to make the cattle baron uncomfortable.

"Maybe I hadn't ought to done it," he grumbled, "but the young squirt riled me for fair. Accused me of cuttin' wire, somethin' I never done in my life. I come nigh to payin' for lettin' my temper get the best of me. He went for his gun. I managed to shoot first, but it was just plumb luck that I nicked him in the arm and caused him to drop his iron before he could pull trigger."

"Yes, I reckon it was lucky you just nicked his arm," Hatfield agreed. "A dead man doesn't make a soft pillow at night."

Wagner looked more uncomfortable. He 'lowed Hatfield might be right.

"Oh, to hell with him," he finished. "Let him go bunk with his nester friends. You ready to ride?"

Many eyes followed Hatfield and Wagner as they rode out of town together. Among the interested eyes were those of Bascomb Price, Sheriff Fulton and Webb Kenton, owner of the Open Diamond O. A little later, the three gathered in the sheriff's office and shut the door.

Bascomb Price instantly exploded, his voice shaking with fear and fury. He glared at Kenton.

"See what comes of shooting that Ranger that day on the train!" he fairly snarled. "See what we're up against? I spotted the big hellion the minute I saw him. That's Bill McDowell's ace man! That's the Lone Wolf!"

Sheriff Fulton's breath exhaled in a reedy sigh. His loose mouth twitched. He glanced wildly around the shuttered room.

Webb Kenton didn't appear particularly impressed. "Well, what of it?" he demanded.

"Well, what of it!" mimicked Price. "You saw what he did to you down at the River, didn't you? Outsmarted the lot of you like you were a pack of sheep. Outsmarted you, outshot you! Killed four men on the boat. Killed Dwyer and Crowley on the trail, and both those fellows were poison with a gun. What of it, eh? I'd rather have the devil on my trail than the Lone Wolf. One thing is sure for certain, he's got to be gotten rid of, if we're to stay here. Oh, I know, it will mean a troop sent down here by McDowell. But I'd rather have the whole Border Batallion, and McDowell himself, than that fellow. It's one thing or the other, he must be gotten rid of, pronto, or we've got to pull out."

"We're not pulling out," Kenton declared.

"Okay. You set up to be salty and smart, Webb. Getting rid of him is your chore."

"I'll handle it," Kenton replied, with vicious emphasis. "It shouldn't be hard. Nobody down here is supposed to know he's a Ranger. I might pick a row with him, and—"

"And die!" Price interrupted. "I know you're good, but he'd make you look like a snail crawling up a slick log. There's not a man in the Southwest can go for a gun, facing him, and live."

"Don't reckon it will be necessary to face him," Kenton said. "Stop shivering, Price. I'll take care of him."

"You'd better," Price warned. "Now, Fulton, *you'd* better appoint Bill Morgan deputy in place of Raines."

"Okay," nodded the sheriff. "Kenton, give me Raines' deputy badge."

"Raines' badge—I haven't got it," Kenton replied.

"You haven't! Where is it, then? Didn't you take it off Raines before you planted him?"

"Hell!" exclaimed Kenton, "now I remember. Raines lent it to Crowley when Crowley rode into the Landing to get the lowdown on when the steamboat would show up. He thought Crowley might need it to get questions answered. It must be in Crowley's pocket. Get it before he's planted."

"Damn it, don't you think I've gone through Crowley's clothes already, and Dwyer's, too?" Sheriff Fulton demanded indignantly. "I took everything off 'em. There was no badge on either of 'em."

Bascomb Price swore a string of oaths.

"Of course you didn't find it on Crowley!" he stormed. "I can tell you where that badge is right now—in Jim Hatfield's pocket. Of all the goddam things to happen. He'll tie that badge up with Raines, sure as hell."

"He can't prove anything," quavered Sheriff Fulton.

"No. But it will start him to thinking. And when that hellion starts thinking, look out!" said Price. "Kenton, you got to work fast."

CHAPTER VIII

OBLIVIOUS OF THE FACT that sentence of death had been passed on him, Jim Hatfield rode on with Arch Wagner. The old cattleman was garrulous, and evidently very proud of his fine spread. He gave Hatfield a prolonged and detailed description of its advantages.

But he knew the cow business and Hatfield found his talk interesting.

"Only one thing bothers me," Wagner remarked at length. "I'm gettin' on in years and I've got nobody to leave all this to when I take the big jump. Never had but one kid, and he died before he growed up. Makes a feller feel sort of lost at times, Hatfield. Makes him wonder if what he's done is worthwhile, after all, when he gets on and there's nobody dependin' on him."

Hatfield glanced at the old man and his green eyes were all kindness.

"A man in your position, suh, has lots of folks depending on him, if he'll only recognize and admit the fact," he said.

Wagner shot him a puzzled look. "What you mean by that, Hatfield?" he asked.

"I mean," Hatfield told him, "that you are a leader in your section. Your neighbors defer to your opinions. You can line them up right. You can help them when they need help. It's to a man's advantage, suh, to have his neighbors friendly to him —all his neighbors."

Wagner tugged his mustache, and seemed at a loss for words. Hatfield tried a shot in the dark.

"I've a notion you might have realized something of that last Election Day," he remarked.

Wagner shot him another look. "The little fellers I never paid much attention to did help the nesters lick us," he grumbled.

"And why were the farmers so anxious to hand you a licking?" Hatfield asked.

"Because they're no good and don't like cowmen," Wagner growled.

"And why don't they like cowmen?" Hatfield persisted. "Wonder if the cowmen ever did anything to them to cause them to dislike cowmen?"

Old Arch rumbled and snorted. "Them horned toads didn't have no business gettin' hold of that land," he declared. "That was always open range."

"Did you really need that land west of the creek to make your spread prosperous and self-sustaining?" Hatfield asked gently.

"I don't see what that's got to do with it," said Wagner.

Hatfield looked contemplative. "On my dad's place, over east of here, we used to raise quite a few pigs," he remarked. "I remember one big hog in particular we had one year. He was a buster. One of the biggest and toughest boars I ever saw. But he was all hog. At feeding time, unless he was watched, he'd shoulder all the little pigs aside and gobble everything he could. But when he was plumb full, he still wasn't satisfied. He'd shove and shoulder, get both feet in the trough, and try to keep the little fellers from getting anything at all. One day, I rec'lect, he got plumb in the trough and lay down."

Hatfield paused, little crinkles at the corners of his eyes.

"And then what happened?" asked Wagner.

"Well," Hatfield finished, "he hadn't even started eating yet that day. And when he shoved everybody else aside and got into the trough, he turned it over. All the food was spilled and every-body, including himself, went hungry."

Arch Wagner flush. His mustache bristled. Then suddenly his fine old mouth quirked at the corners. His snapping eyes twinkled.

"Hatfield," he chuckled, "you're a strange sort of feller. I just met you a couple hours back, but it seems I've knowed you for years. Do you always affect folks this way, first off?"

Hatfield smiled. "It's not always necessary," he replied.

Wagner pondered that one a moment, and decided not to answer. But Hatfield was not displeased. From the look in the cattle baron's eyes, he shrewdly surmised that Arch Wagner was doing some serious thinking.

"Well, here we are at the *casa*," the rancher announced as they turned into the yard and approached the big house in its grove of ancient oaks. "We'll drop our cayuses in the corral and let the wranglers look after 'em. There's Happy Beeler, my range boss, over there. Hi-yuh, Happy, come here."

A mournful-looking individual built something like an ani-mated splinter slouched down the veranda steps.

"Happy, I want you to know Jim Hatfield," Wagner intro-duced the new hand. "He's signed up with us, and he's been tellin' me funny stories."

"That's nice," Beeler said sadly as he shook hands.

"You introduce him to the boys as they drift in," Wagner directed. "After you stow your rig, Hatfield, come up to the house."

Hatfield removed Goldy's saddle and shouldered it. Beeler opened the corral gate and let the big sorrel in to graze. Then he led the way to the bunkhouse.

Outside the building, Hatfield paused an instant. Nearby a fresh-faced young cowboy was industriously stretching a new rope between two trees.

"That's Tommy Eden," Beeler remarked. "Busted his twine

yesterday and's gettin' a new one into shape. Them young squirts are always bustin' somethin', except their necks. Their luck always seems to hold there. There's an empty peg for your saddle. I'm goin' over to the barn. See you later."

After stowing his gear, Hatfield sauntered out of the bunkhouse. He paused to watch the young cowboy shaping his rope.

"Considerable of a chore," he remarked. Eden nodded, and grinned in friendly fashion.

"A chore I always hated," Hatfield continued. "I always used to splice a busted rope if I had both ends. Maybe you got part of your old twine left. Yes? Wait a minute."

He sauntered back into the bunkhouse. A moment later he reappeared, swinging a looped rope in his hand. He passed the broken twine to Eden.

"Maybe you could use this," he remarked seriously. "A feller tied it to something last night he wanted mighty bad to let go of."

With a nod, he passed on to the ranchhouse. Tommy Eden glanced at the coil of rope, started to lay it aside. Suddenly he stiffened, his eyes widened, jerked up and stared after Hatfield's broad back. The color drained from his face, leaving it white to the lips. He dropped the rope as if it had abruptly become red hot, stooped and picked it up again. Then, with a furtive movement, he stuffed the coil inside his shirt, and headed for the bunkhouse in a hurry.

As he mounted the veranda steps, Hatfield glanced over his shoulder, just in time to see Tommy Eden dive into the bunkhouse. He chuckled, his green eyes sunny, and entered the ranchhouse in answer to old Arch's booming invitation to "come on in!"

The big living room of the *casa* was comfortably furnished, with evidence on all sides that its owner was a man of wealth and considerable taste. Hatfield seated himself in an easy chair and rolled a cigarette. Arch Wagner sat by the open window, gazing into the gathering twilight. He nodded to Hatfield, and for some minutes was silent.

"This is the hour I always like best," he said at length. "When the hills are all flamin' purple and the rangeland looks like red wine had been spilled all over it. When things are still and peaceful, and a mite sad. It's a mighty pretty country, Hatfield, especially at this hour. Makes a feller sort of sorry that he wasted so many of them. You get to thinkin' about them things as you grow older."

Jim Hatfield rose to his feet and walked to the window. He, too, gazed upon the glowing beauty of the scene with eyes of appreciation.

Old Arch glanced up at him, standing tall and straight as a young pine of the forest, glorious in his youth and strength. And Arch Wagner's eyes were a trifle wistful. Perhaps he was thinking of his own graying hair and the lines the passing years had etched in his face.

Hatfield suddenly smiled down at him. "Sort of like a man's life, if he's lived it right, suh," he said. "Growing quiet and peaceful and good to look upon. Quiet and peace, and then—the dark."

"And sleep," Wagner said heavily. He was silent again.

"The boys are ridin' in," he said a little later. "About time for chuck."

Shortly afterward, they repaired to the big dining room in answer to the cook's bellow. Here Hatfield met the rest of the Open A hands—a likable bunch, he decided. More than once in the course of the meal he caught young Tommy Eden's glance in his direction. Two other young fellows, who sat on either side of Eden, also appeared to be bothered about something. Hatfield stifled a chuckle.

"I've a notion my hunch is playing straight," he told himself.

When they rose from the table, Arch Wagner beckoned Hatfield to follow him to the living room. The other hands clumped out through the kitchen.

"You might as well bunk here in the house," Wagner told Hatfield. "Take the second room to the right of the stair head. Happy Beeler and a couple of the older fellers sleep here. Tomorrow, you and me will ride over the spread together and you can get a lowdown on things."

"Okay," Hatfield agreed. "I'll slip down to the bunkhouse and get my pouches. Got some spare clothes in 'em."

As Hatfield descended the veranda steps a shadow disengaged itself from a nearby tree trunk. A moment later Hatfield recognized Tommy Eden.

"Feller," Eden whispered, falling in step with the Ranger, "you didn't tell the Old Man where you found that hunk of rope, did you?"

"Nope," Hatfield replied, and waited.

"For Pete's sake, don't!" Eden implored him. "He'd take my hide off, and Smoky's and Toby's, too, if he knew we—we— what happened last night."

Hatfield halted, and turned to face the cowboy.

"Eden," he said, "how did you come to pull that fool prank?"

The cowboy hesitated. "Oh, hell," he said at length, "you got us dead to rights and can twist our tails proper if you're a mind to. It was just a loco notion we got, maybe from too much red-eye. A feller used to set up on that thing and keep watch. One night a couple of weeks back, me and Toby holed up on the bench and dropped a couple of rifle slugs close to him, just to see what he'd do. He liked to jump off, and the way he scooted down that ladder was a caution to cats. I told Webb Kenton about it one day in town, and he sure got a laugh out of it. Last night us fellers were in the Queen High drinkin'. Kenton was there and Chuck Davis, the deputy sheriff. Davis mentioned that the farmers were guardin' their wheat fields and somehow the talk got around to that watch-tower. Webb

Kenton 'lowed somebody had ought to shove the darn thing over, wasn't no sense on the farmers spyin' on every move folks made that way, said it was a sort of insult to the cowmen. Me and Toby and Smoky got to talkin' about it on the way home and figured it would be a good joke on the farmers if we did shove the darn thing over. But we decided it would be easier to rope it and pull it over. Reckon it was lucky we decided to do it that way."

"Damned lucky," Hatfield agreed.

Tommy Eden wiped his brow with his sleeve, although the evening was cool.

"You're darn right," he said. "Golly! I can still hear that dynamite. It made an old man of me before my time. I don't aim to go within a mile of them farm lands again."

"See that you don't and I'll forget the whole thing," Hatfield promised.

"That's fine," Eden replied with a deep sigh of relief. "I'll tell Smoky and Toby so they can sleep tonight. They're scared as I was."

After retiring to his comfortable second-floor room, Hatfield sat for a long time by the open window, smoking and thinking deeply. The moon had risen and the prairie was flooded with silver light. The ranch buildings were dark and silent. Only the occasional stamp or snort of a horse in the nearby corral broke the silence. Then, somewhere, a coyote yipped in an irritated fashion. An owl whined a querulous answer. And from the distant hills came, faint, but clear, the lonely, hauntingly beautiful plaint of a hunting wolf.

Still Hatfield sat by the window, although the other occupants of *casa* and bunkhouse were wrapped in sleep. Suddenly he uttered an exclamation. From his pocket he drew something that glittered in the moonlight. It was the nickel "deputy sheriff" badge he took off the dead owlhoot in the clearing beside the Terlingua Trail. He turned it over in his slim fingers, and gazed at it, the concentration furrow deep between his black brows.

"I wonder," he mused. "I wonder just where this darn thing fits into the tangle? I figured that horned toad stole it somewhere, but I wonder! Could this thing have been given him, or lent him? That deputy sheriff, Raines, I think they called him, who all of a sudden shows up missing. Wonder if he fits in with this somehow? It seems ridiculous, but I wonder. That sheriff feller is a sort of unsavory-looking character, all right. And that lantern-jawed lawyer who got himself elected judge! When I stepped into the sheriff's office today he darn near turned the table over. He kept his face straight, but something sure upset him bad. Just what is going on in this section, anyhow? I sure wish I'd got a look at those two owlhoots the driver and the guards of the gold wagon evidently downed. Those fellers who left the clearing and the wagon to fetch the pack mules must have taken them along, roped to the backs of their horses, chances are. Now why were they so anxious to dispose of them, instead of dumping them out of the wagon there in the clearing? 'Pears they didn't hanker for anybody to get a look at them. Well, it's a funny mess, but I'm beginning to get another hunch. Maybe I'll be able to tie onto something tomorrow when I ride the range with Wagner. And now I figure a little shut-eye is in order."

Right after breakfast the following morning, Hatfield and Wagner started on their ride. They worked west, at first, reached the banks of Terloga Creek and rode beside the hurrying water of the broad stream. West of the creek were the farm lands. Wagner glowered at the taut strands of rusty wire.

"That's what's ruinin' the cow country," he growled.

Hatfield gazed across the creek. Beyond the wire were great strands of wheat, corn, soy beans and alfalfa.

"Mighty good forage there," he commented, inconsequentially. "A field like that would keep a cowman from going busted in bad blizzard weather when the cows can't graze."

Old Arch shot him a hostile glance. "We don't have many blizzards down here," he grunted.

"But when we do, it's a lulu," Hatfield replied. "Reckon blizzards have cost you considerable at one time or another, suh."

Wagner 'lowed it was so. His eyes rested on the green fields beyond the wire.

"Those fellers work hard to make a living," Hatfield remarked. "And they don't get over much at that. I sure slept well in that good bed last night, suh. A nice big room, too. And your *casa* is a mighty nice place to live in. Cool in summer. Warm and comfortable in winter. Nice to be well fixed and not have to worry about anything. Not even any kids to worry about —whether they're going to get an education, and the other things due them. Some folks have lots of kids, which is a fine thing, too. But they want those kids to be happy and live well, and get out of life what they should get by working hard and living square and being considerate of other folks. If your kid had lived, suh, I reckon he'd have had everything he needed, and a chance to get started right in life."

Old Arch tugged his mustache, squirmed in his saddle. Suddenly he whirled about to face his new hand.

"Hatfield," he rumbled, "you don't have to go and make me feel like a goddamned horned toad, or like that big hog you were tellin' me about yesterday."

Jim Hatfield glanced down at him, his eyes mirthful. "Now, suh," he protested, "I wouldn't think of doing anything like that. After all, suh, I'm working for you. I'm just a jigger that you gave a job to when he was looking for one."

Arch Wagner snorted. "I'm beginnin' to wonder about that," he declared. "I've had lots of hands workin' for me in my time, but I never before had one talk to me like I was a little squirt perched on a stool with a dunce cap on my head. Just who in hell are you, Hatfield?"

"Told you my name, suh," the Ranger replied. "It's the one I was born to. And I reckon before the week's over you'll agree I'm a cowhand, a sort of one, anyhow."

Satisfied to let the seed he planted in the old cattleman's mind do its growing for a while, Hatfield adroitly steered the conversation into other channels. Wagner was a real cowman and he became animated as he explained the workings of his big spread. Hatfield nodded and agreed, dropping a word now and then where it would do the most good and tend to draw Wagner out.

"Mighty fine-looking cows in that bunch over there," he suddenly remarked. "Improved stock, I see."

"That's right," replied Wagner. "I don't have any other kind. None better. But," his face darkened, "if things keep on going as they have been, I won't have any kind. Hatfield, I tell you they're stealin' me blind! That's one reason why I'm on the prod against the farmers. If they ain't in cahoots with those goddam Scarlet Riders, they ain't above lendin' 'em a helpin' hand now and then."

"What makes you say that, suh?" Hatfield asked gravely.

"Well," Wagner explained defensively, "there wasn't any Scarlet Riders till they moved in. Hadn't been any rustlin' to speak of in this section for years. Then about a year and a half back it started and has been goin' on ever since, and gettin' worse all the time. All the stealin's are run west into the hills, crossin' the nesters' holdin's to the north of here. We can't patrol those holdin's without having trouble with the nesters, so once the owlhoots slide 'em across Terloga Creek they're settin' pretty. They don't have to look out for patrols. They just keep on shovin' 'em fast in case anybody is on the trail. And once they get into the hills to the west, the cows are as good as gone."

"They can't run them out any other way except through the western hill country?" Hatfield asked.

"Nope," Wagner replied. "The only way to go south except by circlin' through those hills is by way of Persimmon Gap through the Santiagos. And for mile after mile the goin' is so steep that a herd can't move faster than a slow walk. Any loco jigger tryin' to shove a herd through the Gap would be run down pronto. But through the western hills it's different. Trails there, trails the Indians used to use, and the damned wideloopers seem to know 'em all."

"And you haven't been able to track them through the hills?"

Wagner shook his head. "It's one gosh-awful mess over there," he explained. "Canyons and ridges and draws and gulleys runnin' every darn way. If you're not familiar with them, you get lost in no time. We've tried to track 'em through there time and again, but we always lose the trail. Once they cross Terloga Creek and get onto the rocky ground to the north and west of here they always give us the slip. And they're smart operators with plenty of wrinkles on their horns. They don't go in for big herds that handle slow. They seldom knock off more'n a hundred head at a time. Fellers that know their business can move a small herd like that mighty fast. And it don't take many of them small herds to mount up to a big one."

Hatfield nodded his understanding. Such steady, methodical robbing meant in the end a greater loss to the rancher than the once-in-a-great-while running-off a large herd. No cowman could stand it.

"No, they can't go through the Gap," Wagner repeated. "And if they did try to run 'em south, they'd have to pass over Webb Kenton's holdin's and mighty close to his ranchhouse. And Kenton keeps a sharp lookout. He's lost stock, too, of course, but they run 'em north and west same as they do off my spread and the ones farther to the east."

"But your losses have been the heaviest?" Hatfield questioned.

"Yes," Wagner replied. "I'm placed just right for the hellions." He glowered westward. Hatfield let that angle pass for the moment. Nor was he inclined to agree with Wagner's contention that the stolen cattle could not be tracked through the western hills. He was already forming a plan relative to that matter.

They rode on steadily for a couple of hours, constantly veering to the south. Finally, ahead loomed a tall and broad ridge with Terloga Creek washing its base as it flowed westward toward the hills.

Wagner jerked his thumb toward the ridge.

"Down the other side of the sag is Webb Kenton's spread," he announced. "I owned that land once but I sold out to Kenton, figurin' I was puttin' over a good deal. But it was Kenton what was puttin' one over. Like to see how he did it? I'll tell you about it as we ride over the hill."

As they rode up the long slope, Hatfield again heard the story with variations of Kenton's shrewdness and the tapping of the underground waters of Terloga Creek.

But not until they rode down the far side of the sag did he fully appreciate the Open Diamond O owner's sagacity and unusual ability.

"There she is," said Wagner, gesturing at the torrent of sparkling water pouring from a wide and high opening in the face of the cliff. "Hundreds of times, I reckon, I rode past them dadblamed cliffs and saw the ferns and lichens growin' on 'em when everything else was dry and burned up. And I never figured what it meant.

"But Kenton figured what it meant, mighty fast," he continued with a grimace. "He knew there must be moisture seepin' out of the cliff to cause that truck to grow there. He figured there'd be plenty of water not far behind them cracked rocks. He was right. And look how the jigger spreads the water over the land. Smart? Instead of one crik runnin' along, he's got half a dozen tumblin' out over his range. Plumb perfect!"

Wordless, Hatfield stared at the exhibition of more than a little engineering skill and knowledge spread before his eyes.

At the base of the cliff the rushing water had scored a deep catch basin and channel. But a few hundred yards from the base, an astoundingly clever system of dams set at angles had been constructed. A portion of the water was shunted off in various channels prepared to receive it. As Wagner said, Kenton had contrived a number of streams to flow across his land and fill his water holes.

But it was the construction of the dams that interested Hatfield most. They were contrived with cribbings of stout timbers. The cribbings were filled with earth and stone, providing an efficient barrier that turned the water as desired.

"Most jiggers would have just built a dam across the main creek and conveyed the water over the land by a system of irrigation ditches," Hatfield mused. "But that gent, plumb full of savvy, contrived to make the water do the work itself. He took advantage of the natural slope of the land from the cliff face and formed artificial brooks. Unlike irrigation ditches, they don't silt up but scour out their own channels. In consequence, the flow is never retarded. Smart! Plumb smart!"

He raised his eyes as he spoke and stared southward toward the distant and unseen Rio Grande. He glanced back again at the cunningly contrived cribbings. The concentration furrow was deep between his black brows and his eyes had subtly changed color until they were as coldly gray as the beetling cliff walls rising on either side of the rushing water. One hand slid into his side pocket and fingered the mysterious deputy sheriff's badge.

CHAPTER IX

A BUSY WEEK FOLLOWED for Hatfield and the rest of the Open A hands. The roundup season was approaching and there was much to do in addition to getting the big trail herd together. Very quickly, Arch Wagner was convinced that he had not in many a long day hired such a tophand as Jim Hatfield proved to be.

"I can't give that big jigger orders," Happy Beeler, the range boss, complained sadly. "He knows more about it all than I do and he's always one jump ahead of me."

"Leave him alone," growled Wagner. "He knows what to do and he'll do it. He's first class at book work, too. The other night I was tryin' to straighten out my papers and having a hell of a time. He listened to me cuss a while, then he grinned that funny quirkin' grin of his and took over. In a jiffy, he had everything straightened out and in tip-top shape. Showed me where I'd been makin' mistakes, and did it in a way that made it look like he was just askin' advice. He's a whizzer. And somehow," he added reflectively, "I've a notion he's a heap more used to givin' orders than takin' 'em. He's sure got a way of bringin' a man around to his way of thinkin'. And does it so smooth, you don't realize what's goin' on."

"You figger he's been a range boss somewhere?" Beeler asked.

"Uh-huh," Wagner replied dryly. "I've a notion he's been a range boss of some sort or another on a mighty big range. He's sure puzzlin'."

Beeler nodded agreement, and predicted mournfully: "He won't stay. His sort is always on the move."

"Maybe not," Wagner admitted, "but he's takin' hold here like he has a real interest in the business. Might fool you. I sure hope so."

The following afternoon, while Hatfield was giving Wagner a little help with his books, Beeler entered looking more lugubrious than usual.

"Well," he said, "they got away with better'n fifty head last night, from the northeast pasture."

Old Arch raised both fists in the air and swore till the rafters creaked.

"Are you sure?" he demanded. "They didn't stray somewhere?"

"Of course I'm sure," declared Beeler. "Wasn't any reason for those cows to stray. Good water. Good grass. They were there yesterday morning. They ain't there now. Tracks led straight west, horses' tracks, too. Same old story, boss."

"You try to follow the tracks?"

Beeler shrugged his scrawny shoulders. "What was the use?" he asked. "I tell you the tracks led west for the hills. How many times have we followed tracks into that mess of canyons and gulleys? Always the same. Lost 'em over there. Besides, I was by myself. What good would it have done me to catch up with the hellions? I couldn't have done anything. Just got blowed out of my hull if I'd tried it. But," he added, "if I'd figured there was a chance to run 'em down, I might have took a chance. I just didn't see no sense in it, that's all."

Wagner grunted and growled, and swore some more. He was forced to admit there was sense in what Beeler said.

Jim Hatfield spoke for the first time. "It rained early last night," he said thoughtfully. "Ground should have been soft. Maybe there would be a chance to tail them. Don't you think it's worth trying, suh?"

"You're right it is!" Wagner declared vigorously. "Happy, several of the boys are makin' some fence repairs on the south corral. Round 'em up and we'll ride over to the pasture and see what we can do."

Ten minutes later the group, eight strong, was riding swiftly into the northeast.

They reached the pasture about midafternoon. A single glance told Hatfield that Beeler had made no mistake. The bedding down place near the waterhole was plainly discernible. So were the tracks of cows and horses leading away from the pasture in a westerly direction.

"Let's go," he said, taking his place at the head of the column. "Keep in single file so as not to cut up the ground more than necessary."

In the vicinity of the pasture the trail was plain enough. Farther out on the prairie where the grass was taller, it was not so easy to follow. But Hatfield had little trouble holding to the right course. Mile after mile they covered till they reached the east bank of Terloga Creek. The trail ran straight to the water's edge. Without pausing they sent their horses splashing across the wide and shallow stream. But on the far bank, Hatfield called a halt. He sat staring at the multitude of prints scoring the soft surface of the west bank.

"They sure did a heap of milling here," he remarked.

"Reckon they stopped to let the critters drink," Wagner hazarded.

"Perhaps," Hatfield agreed, "but I wonder why they didn't wait on the east bank to let them drink if they needed water?"

Nobody could provide an answer. Nor could Hatfield himself, for that matter. He spoke to Goldy and rode on. Soon the ground became more broken and stonier, the going harder.

The hoofs of the cattle left little imprint, but the irons of the horses still left visible markings.

But now the hills were close, a wild and weird jumble of spires and cones and towering cliffs slashed by the dark mouths of canyons into any of which the herd might have vanished. Flanking the base of the hills and nearly a half mile in width was what appeared to be a stretch of black stone where grew no tree, shrub or blade of grass.

"See?" Arch Wagner remarked sententiously, pointing to the forbidding expanse.

Hatfield whistled under his breath. "Lava beds," he said. "Like those east of Mount Pisgah in California and around the Ashes Mountains northwest of here."

Ten minutes more and they were on the clinker, which proved to be rough, jagged and hard as iron. Not a sign of the passage of cattle or horses was to be seen. Even Hatfield admitted himself defeated. A regiment of cavalry could have passed that way without leaving a trace.

The sun was low in the sky, the shadows lengthening. Already the canyon mouths were swathed in gloom. Hatfield shook his head.

"Too late to do anything more," he said. "We might as well turn around and head for home. But, suh," he told Wagner," if you don't mind, I'd like to ride over this way early tomorrow and give those canyons a closer going-over."

"Suit yourself," grunted the ranchowner. "If you can find *anything,* you'll do more than anybody else has—go ahead."

They headed back the way they came. Hatfield was silent, giving his whole attention to the trail. A quarter of a mile or so from the creek bank, where the ground was soft, he suddenly pulled up.

"Wait a minute," he said and dismounted. For minutes he studied the surface of the trail.

"This is a funny one," he said slowly. "Unless my eyes are

going back on me, they ran some of those cows back to the creek."

"What the hell!" sputtered Wagner. "That's the locoest soundin' thing you've said yet."

"Come down and see," Hatfield replied.

Still muttering, old Arch Wagner unforked and joined Hatfield. A moment later he swore louder than before.

"Son, I'm damned if you ain't right," he said. "A lot of these hoof marks do point toward the creek. Now what in hell does this mean? What did those owlhoots turn the herd, or part of it, back this way?"

"I don't know," Hatfield admitted, "but it's interesting."

"Maybe they figured they needed more water," one of the hands guessed.

"Could be," Hatfield agreed, "but it would be a darn funny thing for experienced cowmen to do."

"Maybe their conscience hurt 'em and they decided to bring some of 'em back," Happy Beeler remarked mournfully. The observation was doubtless intended to be humorous, but nobody laughed.

"You got darn queer notions about bein' funny!" snorted old Arch. "Conscience! Those buzzards ain't got no more conscience than a stampedin' cow. Come on, let's go home!"

The following morning Hatfield rode into the hills. He spent most of the day combing the canyons and draws, with no results. Finally in disgust he hooked a leg over the saddle horn, rolled a cigarette and sat smoking and gazing toward the smudge against the southern sky that marked the site of Marton.

"I think I'll just amble down there and give that pueblo the once-over," he told Goldy. "Might pick up a loose end there. Certainly not tieing onto any here. The hellions could run that herd in here and not leave a trace. The damndest hole-in-the-wall country I ever saw. Old Arch is right, though. It would be possible to circle around to the south and reach the Rio Grande, or drive west into New Mexico. The whole terrain is made to order for rustlers and other hell-raisers. I can ride around here for a month and not stumble onto anything except through sheer luck. And luck isn't much to go on in this business. Let's go, horse. Feeling mighty empty, too, and we should both be able to tie onto a surroundin' of chuck down there, anyhow."

Upon reaching Marton, Hatfield found quarters for Goldy at a livery stable down an alley. Then he sought out the Queen High saloon. Sheriff Craig Fulton, the owner, was standing at the far end of the bar. He greeted Hatfield jovially, evidently striving for the role of the urbane host. Hatfield looked him over more carefully than he had at their first meeting. He took in the sheriff's fleshy face, blue-black where it was shaven, his shifty eyes set deep in rolls of fat, and his mouth, the muscles of which could not quite keep it in place. He noticed that the sheriff also had nicked teeth. These obvious disadvantages he did his best to hide by a Falstaffian joviality—for Sheriff Fulton was growing stout.

A few minutes later Judge Bascomb Price came in. He greeted Hatfield with dignified courtesy and congratulated him on going to work for Arch Wagner.

"Not a better man in the section," the judge declared sonorously. "We need more citizens like Arch Wagner."

Hatfield nodded agreement and repaired to a nearby table and ordered a meal. The judge, after a low-voiced conversation with the sheriff, took his leave, nodding to Hatfield on his way out. Sheriff Fulton busied himself at the bar, apparently forgetting all about Hatfield. The Ranger enjoyed a leisurely meal, had a drink after he finished eating and then left the Queen High. Fulton did not even glance in his direction. He wandered about town, visiting various places. Several times he overheard groups discussing the Scarlet Riders and the rustling that plagued the section, but learned nothing of value. About midnight he headed for the livery stable and bed, having engaged a room over the stalls. As he was passing under a large tree that grew almost in front of the stable, a slight sound caused him to glance up, but just an instant too late. Something swished down from the dark cavern of leaves and branches above. A close loop dropped over his head and shoulders and was instantly jerked tight, pinning his arms to his sides. Men swarmed out of the shadows.

Hatfield could not move his arms, but nevertheless he put up a terrific fight, kicking, butting, lunging with his big shoulders. He had two men on the ground and was going for a third when a gun barrel crashed against his skull and he dropped senseless.

"Blazes! what a man!" panted a big fellow, sheathing the gun he had used as a club. "Seems a damn shame to do in a jigger like this!"

"Shut up!" mouthed a companion, spitting out blood and a tooth. "If he'd knocked *your* jaw clean around to the back of your neck, you wouldn't think so damn well of him. Boost him up onto the horse and tie him tight—don't take any chances with him. Gabe, you got his guns? Okay. No, you can't have 'em. Irons like those are distinctive. Put 'em out of sight and bring 'em along. Let's get going now before somebody comes nosin' around."

CHAPTER X

When Jim Hatfield regained consciousness he was roped fast to a speeding horse. His hands weer securely tied and he was blindfolded. For some minutes he remained as he was, slumped forward, his face buried in the horse's coarse mane, a pounding ache in his head and red flashes wavering before his bandaged eyes, a crawling nausea in his stomach.

Gradually his head cleared. The pain and the retching sickness lessened. Both were replaced by a seething anger directed at himself.

"Caught settin'!" he muttered bitterly. "Walked smack into a trap! Knew damn well those hellions would be out to even up the score and walked into it like I was blindfolded. Guess some folks never learn!"

For a little longer he lay slumped forward, trying to tie up the loose ends of recent happenings. He could distinguish the hoofbeats of a number of horses other than the one he was roped to. A mutter of conversation was going on between his captors. He strained his ears to catch what was said.

"When do you figure the Boss will get there?" a voice asked.

"Dunno, soon as he can make it, I reckon," another replied. "Frank hightailed with the word we'd grabbed this buzzard. We'll corral this feller and then sift sand. We got a chore to do and it can't wait. We'll have to hump ourselves to make it."

"I hanker for a mite of coffee," growled another voice. "My head's splittin' wide open. That hellion nearly busted my jaw."

"It's liable to split a heap wider if the Boss gets up to the north first and has to wait on us," the first speaker replied. "But I reckon he'll feel pretty good over us gettin' this feller. Maybe we can take time out to boil a pot. I could stand a swaller myself. Sift sand, you jugheads, we got a ways yet to go."

"I don't see no sense in packin' this buzzard into the hills," the other voice complained querulously. "Why not drill him now and get it over with?"

"You know what our orders were—to corral this feller and pack him to the hangout," the first speaker said. "Reckon the Boss wants to talk to him first, maybe ask him a few questions; the Boss is good at gettin' answers, even from fellers who don't want to talk. Anyhow, orders is orders and we're takin' 'em. The Boss knows what he's about."

Hatfield listened attentively, hoping they would call the Boss by name, but they did not. They fell silent and quickened the horses' pace. Hatfield decided he'd played 'possum in his uncomfortable position long enough. He began groaning and twisting in his bonds, slowly returning to consciousness. He was cramped and wanted to straighten up but preferred that his captors did not learn that he had been eavesdropping on their talk. A moment later he clawed himself erect with his bound hands and sat swaying drunkenly.

"Comin' out of it, eh?" said the voice of the man who appeared to be in charge of the group. "Well, just sit tight and keep your mouth shut if you don't wanta dive back in again. No funny business, now; we ain't to be fooled with."

Hatfield took the hint and remained silent, but his keen ears were working overtime. He judged from the sound of the horses' irons and their labored breathing, and from his position in the saddle, that the trail they were following was a steep and rocky one, winding, too. The hoofbeats seemed to echo back from the left, which would tend to indicate they were climbing a mountain track with a slope or a cliff on one side and probably with a drop into a canyon or gorge on the other.

Another half an hour or so of climbing and the trail levelled off. Abruptly the horses swerved to the left and began floundering through thick brush. Hatfield could feel twigs brushing his clothes and more than once a branch whipped across his face. The hoofbeats, too, were muffled, as if by soft ground or a carpet of mold.

Once again their course levelled and the irons rang on hard soil. Another ten minutes and the troop halted. Hatfield felt hands fumbling with the cords that bound him to the stirrup straps. The binding cramp about his legs and ankles was removed.

"Okay," said a voice, "you can unfork now."

Hatfield obeyed, awkwardly and stiffly, an unseen hand aiding him to descend from the hull. His legs were so numb he could hardly stand; but as he stumbled, hands gripped him and urged him forward. He felt that he was climbing a gentle slope. Then his footsteps rang back hollow echoes. A moment later he was jerked to a halt. The cords were loosed from his wrists and the bandage removed from his eyes. He stood blinking in a glow of light.

Presently his vision cleared and he saw that he was in a rock-walled chamber perhaps twenty feet square. It was lighted by several lanterns suspended from pegs, and a blazing fire, the smoke of which evidently found its way out through crevices in the rocky roof, for the entrance to what was apparently a cave or mine tunnel was barred by a closed door of roughly hewn timbers. Another and smaller door of planks showed in the far wall, hinged to beams set in the stone. Both planks and timbers were worn and weatherbeaten, and the padlock that secured the inner door was on an old pattern.

Rifles were stacked against the wall. Guns, a goodly number of them, hung from pegs driven into the stone. Among them Hatfield noted his own cartridge belts and holstered sixes.

Grouped about the fire were half a dozen men, all wearing red masks. Presently a big, burly individual, evidently the leader of the band, brought Hatfield a cup of steaming coffee liberally spiked from a black bottle.

"Here," he rumbled, "this'll put hair on your belly. You may be all wrong, from our way of looking at it, but you're a first-rate fightin' man, and I cotton to a good fightin' man no matter who or what he is."

Hatfield gratefully accepted the cup and drank the hot liquid with avidity. Under its stimulus his head cleared still further and he felt renewed strength flowing through his veins.

"Okay," the masked leader said as Hatfield handed back the empty cup with a nod of thanks. "Now we'll stow you away for a spell. The Boss will want to have a little gab with you when he shows up in the mornin'. I'm scairt it's curtains for you, feller. Don't nobody get in the Boss' way and not pay for it mighty heavy. Shove him in there, Cart."

The last was addressed to a man with thick, bowed shoulders who had swung open the inner door, disclosing a dark interior. A moment later Hatfield found himself in total darkness as the door banged shut and the padlock clicked.

In the outer room voices rumbled for a few minutes, then departing footsteps sounded on the rock floor. The ponderous outer door closed with a crash and there was silence broken only by the faint crackling of the dying fire.

Without delay, Hatfield began exploring his prison. His tobacco and papers had been left untouched, also matches in a tightly corked bottle. He struck one and glanced about. The room was rock-walled like the one he had just left but considerably smaller. In the far wall from the entrance, he discovered a third door, hasped and padlocked. The room was totally devoid of furnishings. He returned to the entrance and tried the door with his shoulder. It creaked and the hasp jangled but resisted his efforts. It was constructed of heavy planks and undoubtedly too sturdy to be forced by his unaided strength. And there was nothing at hand with which he might batter it down. His knife had been taken and his guns, hanging in the outer room, might as well have been in Marton for all the good they were likely to do him. He sat down on the rock floor with his back against the door, rolled a cigarette and did some hard thinking.

Hatfield knew he was on a tough spot. It was logical to believe that he was in the hands of the notorious Scarlet Riders and could expect but short shrift after the Boss, whoever he might be, showed up. He wondered if the bunch had spotted him for a Ranger. There was something on which to base the hypothesis. Had the attack on him been motivated only by revenge for his foiling the attempted robbery of the river steamer, a quick knife thrust would have been the logical procedure. But if they knew he was a Ranger, a more subtle method of doing away with him was likely. Killing a Ranger was something even the most ruthless outfit was reluctant to do. It would mean a troop in the section and a relentless pursuit of the killers. But causing a Ranger merely to vanish, with no evidence as to what became of him, and none to link his abductors with the act, was something else again. And there was the time element to consider. It would be quite a while before Captain McDowell was convinced that his Lieutenant and ace-man had really been done away with. And by that time the bunch might well be able to cover their tracks or leave for parts unknown.

Be that as it might, Jim Hatfield earnestly desired to be elsewhere when the Boss showed up at the cave. But how to be elsewhere was the question, a sizeable one.

Pinching out his cigarette, he stood up and lighted another match and proceeded to give the door another careful once-over.

He was about to give up in despair when he made an important discovery. The timber casing in which the door was set was much older than the door itself. The wood was rotten, worm-eaten and crumbling. The hinges were held in place by three stout screws. Hatfield tentatively set a finger-nail in one of the slots. He uttered an exultant exclamation. To all appearances the screws had become somewhat loosened due to the decay of the timber. With something to use for a screwdriver he might be able to loosen them. But what the devil could he use? His knife had been taken from him and there was nothing in the room that would serve. He fingered his belt buckle. The rounded edge was too thick to fit into the slots.

Abruptly he had an inspiration. He fumbled at a cunningly concealed secret pocket in the broad leather belt. From it he drew his Ranger badge, the familiar silver star set on a silver circle. The badge was backed with steel. And the curved rim slipped easily into the screw slot. By God! it might work! He carefully fitted the rim into the slot, held it firmly in place and put forth a steady torsion. His heart beat faster as he felt the screw move. A few minutes of work and he was able to draw it from the wood. Feverishly he set to work on a second screw.

But all did not come forth as easily as had the first one. Before the last screw of the lower hinge was out, Hatfield's fingers were bruised and raw. He was trembling in every limb and the rim of the badge was bent and gashed. For a few minutes he leaned against the door jamb, breathing hard while his strength returned. Then he grasped the loose upper hinge and pulled hard.

The door sagged away from the jamb, enough to enable him to get his fingers into the crack and secure a good hold on the planks. He wrenched and tugged with all his strength. The padlock held firm, but the hasp bent, the door swung around and he had an opening through which he could force his body.

The fire had burned down to glowing coals. The outer room

was swathed with shadows. Hatfield struck another match, located one of the lanterns and touched the flame to the wick. It burned with a steady glow. He lighted another and glanced about. His holstered guns still hung on the peg. To secure them was the work of a moment. He made sure they were loaded and in perfect working condition. With the big Colts buckled around his waist, he felt much better. Then he proceeded to take thorough stock of his surroundings. First he examined the outer door and gave it up as hopeless. It was constructed of massive timbers and barred and bolted on the outside. Foolish to even try to batter it down. He glanced at the glowing coals of the fire and gave that up, too.

"Take a week to burn through the darn thing," he muttered disgustedly, his gaze roving about the chamber.

He noted things he had overlooked during his brief stay in the outer room. Built along the walls were bunks. In one corner was a supply of staple provisions. On a crude bench was a pail of water. He found coffee still warm in the coffeepot and drank a cup thirstily. Then he continued to survey his surroundings. He quickly revised his first estimate of the chamber. It was not a cave, but had been hollowd out by the hand of man. Marks of tools were plain on the rock wall.

"An old Spanish mine, that's what it is," he muttered. "Those hellions must have stumbled onto it and converted it into a hole-up. A good one, all right, well hid back in the hills, doubtless."

The discovery was interesting but of little help in his present predicament, so far as he could see. Looked like he had but two alternatives to choose from. He could wait for the outlaws to return and give battle against heavy odds. Or he could try and barricade the entrance and withstand a siege. Neither offered a satisfactory solution. He prowled about in hope of finding something that would be to his advantage. Holding a lantern aloft, he peered into the smaller room that had been his prison on the chance he might have overlooked something of importance. His gaze centered on the padlocked inner door and suddenly he exclaimed aloud. If his surmise was correct and he was in the storeroom or living quarters of an old mine, beyond that locked door should be the mine tunnel. He forced his way through the narrow crack between the jamb and the sagging door and approached the farther barrier.

The lock was old, apparently of cast iron, and looked strong. And he didn't feel up to another battle with the screws that held the hasp in place. But now there was an easier way. He drew one of his guns, stepped back a couple of paces and let drive at the lock.

The heavy bullet smashed the rusty iron to bits. Hatfield raised the catch, released the bolt and tugged at the door. It swung open on screaming hinges and before him was a dark passage. It was the mine tunnel.

Hatfield hesitated a moment, trying to decide to what use to put his discovery. The tunnel was likely to be but a *cul de sac,* but his experience with such bores was that frequently ventillating shafts led to the outer air. One might prove a feasible exit. He resolved to take the chance. After all, he could hardly worsen matters, and it would be a tough chore for the outlaws to root him out of the workings of the old mine. If nothing else, he would gain time, and under the circumstances time was a highly important factor. He returned to the large chamber and secured a second lantern, making sure its bowl was filled to capacity with oil. Then, after another cup of coffee, he set out.

The floor of the tunnel was smooth and almost level, the walls arching a foot or so over his head. He noted that the air, while close and heavy, was fresh enough—evidence that somewhere there was a second opening. He struck a match and watched the flame. It wavered back toward the chamber. Air draws inward, not outward. There was another opening somewhere. With renewed hope he trudged on through the darkness and the awful silence that pressed in upon him like a living thing.

Soon the passage took a sharp turn. Then it was bisected by another. Hatfield hesitated, then decided to keep on in what appeared to be the main gallery of the old mine. Soon there was another change of direction and another cross tunnel. He seemed to be in a stone labyrinth which led to nowhere. He noted one discouraging factor. The slope of the passage, while gentle, was persistently downward suggesting that it plunged into the bowels of the earth without any second opening to the outer air. Then, after what seemed a very long time, the corridor levelled off. It still turned and twisted, with bisecting passages, changing its course so frequently that soon he was utterly confused and not at all sure he hadn't turned into some side tunnel. He began to experience an eerie feeling that he was continually travelling in a circle and getting nowhere at all. He knew well that he was hopelessly lost with scant chance of retracing his steps to the outer chamber. Not that he had any desire to do so. He resolved to keep on going till he dropped.

After another hour of weary trudging along the echoing gallery he became conscious of a low, persistent sound. At first, he thought it was but the blood roaring in his veins or a ringing of the ears set up by the heavy atmosphere. But the sound steadily increased in volume, grew from a murmur to a deep droning, swelled to a plaint interspersed by uncanny shrieks and wail. Hatfield was at a loss to account for the origin of the tumult.

Gradually it seemed to him that the black darkness ahead was graying. At first, he thought it but a figment of overwrought imagination, but the faint light increased until he could make out the sides of the corridor. And abruptly he realized that he was no longer following one of the mine bores. The passage was undoubtedly of natural origin, apparently hollowed out by the action of water in some past age.

Hatfield experienced a feeling of exultation. His experience was that underground water eventually reaches the surface. Which would presage an opening to the open air somewhere ahead. He hurried on, breathing hard.

The ghostly sounds increased in volume till the rock walls seemed to quiver under their impact. A moment later and he saw that the tunnel had come to an end.

But what an end! Hatfield's scalp prickled as he stared at the unearthly scene before him.

The tunnel opened into a mighty chasm in the black rock, jagged and torn and splintered, as if in some dim distant age of the past a terrific lightning bolt had cleaved the granite cliffs like a flaming sword of vengeance, leaving this ghastly wound in the earth's breast. The opposite cliff of the chasm was swathed in blackness and the exact width of the gulf was impossible to determine.

Hatfield glanced up. Far, far above, fully two thousand feet, he estimated, was a narrow ribbon of blue sky from which heavy dregs of light seeped to the depths in which he stood. The gloom of the chasm was the gloom of a closely shuttered room in the daytime.

How far downward it extended from the lip of the corridor he could not tell, but the impenetrability of the gloom suggested tremendous depths.

And rising from the lip of the corridor, and of a width almost as great was a stupendous natural bridge of dark stone.

Up and up soared the mighty arch, its titanic curve suggestive of Bifrost Bridge, sharp as a sword edge, that spans the Gulf of Death to Valhalla. Beyond the apex of the arch the far cliff evidently overhung, shutting off even the feeble light that struggled down from the heights. The bridge beyond this point was invisible, giving the impression of a prodigious half-arc suspended in the arms of the darkness.

Down the gulf great winds dashed and roared, driving misty

wreaths and clouds of vapor before them, until the cyclopean span hummed and moaned like a giant harp. Wailings and shriekings arose as the gusts tore through crevices in the splintered stone; and the echoing cliffs magnified the sound a hundredfold, until it seemed a concourse of demons from the Pit were holding high revel in the darksome cleft.

For long minutes Jim Hatfield stood staring at the awful scene. Then he shrugged his shoulders and stepped boldly on the causeway of the bridge.

Instantly he was exposed to the full force of the wind. He reeled, staggered, kept his balance with difficulty. Then, bending almost double, he crept cautiously up the gentle slope of the arc, holding the flickering lantern well in front of him, examining each foot of the stone before he trusted his weight upon it.

"Lucky I got a lantern with a globe instead of a torch," he muttered. "The wind would blow a torch out in no time."

He had covered much more than a hundred paces before he reached the apex of the arch. Here the gloom lessened somewhat and he quickened his pace. Fifty yards farther on, however, just before he reached the downward curve of the span, he halted abruptly. At his feet was a crevice fully fifteen feet in width and extending downward into the mass of the rock for an unknown distance.

Hatfield crept to the splintered edge of the bridge and gazed downward into depth upon vertiginous depth that seemed to extend to the heart of the earth itself. In the gulf moved vast mist shadows, like to those cast by the wings of the Birds of Eternity, which, say the Arabs, are so great the earth can cower beneath them like a nestling.

Shaken, giddy, he moved back from the edge and stood on the firmer lip of the crevice in the bridge floor, measuring the width with his eye, carefully examining to the best of his ability in the uncertain light, the condition of the ground on the other side of the cleft. For he had resolved to take the hazardous risk of jumping the crevice rather than try to find his way back to the outlaws' hangout and the almost certain fate that awaited him there. Better to gamble on the problematical chance of escape. At the worst it would mean a quick end.

The distance, he decided, was indeed not more than fifteen feet. In his college days, Hatfield had jumped more than twenty feet, but certainly not under such awesome conditions. All that lay before him was a splintered, jagged lip of rock in a half darkness of shifting shadows, and a hurricane of gusty wind tearing and thrusting at him, a gulf of unknown depth to clear, and a landing place of broken, uneven stone. He drew a deep breath and hesitated.

But the only alternative was to retrace his steps, if he could, to the owlhoots' hangout with almost certain death awaiting him at the end of the wearisome tramp. Yes, better to take the chance. Without doubt the corridor continued on the far side of the gulf and there was always the probability that it eventually reached the open air again. He had been encouraged for some time by a steady upward trend of the grade. Yes, it was better to take a chance.

Regretfully he set the lantern aside, comforting himself with the thought that the oil must be pretty nigh gone. He retraced his steps a few yards, took another deep breath and ran forward at full speed.

The mighty wind whipped and tore at him. The wild storm voices, set to the deep undertone of the broken span that hummed like a gigantic tuning fork, howled a warning and a threat. The shadows crawled and shifted. The crumbling rock turned beneath his feet.

He reached the lip of the crevice and sprang wildly out into the dizzy air. A horrible sense of despair seized his brain as he realized he had jumped short.

CHAPTER XI

For what seemed untold ages, Hatfield shot through the screaming air and plunged downward, his clutching hands outstretched. As he hurtled into the depths, his arms and his hands slammed against the opposite lip of the cleft with numbing force. The fingers of one hand closed about a knob of rock and stopped his downward progress with a jerk that almost tore his arm from the socket.

For an instant that was an eternity he swung wildly to and fro, with the clawing shadows all around him and the black depths beneath. Then by a prodigious effort he managed to stretch his other arm far enough to grasp a second knob of stone. He hung gasping, gathering his strength. Then he exerted his powerful muscles to the full and gradually drew himself up until his breast was resting on the rough stone of the bridge floor. Another writhe and struggle and he lay at full length upon the vibrating causeway, shaking, his nerves tautened to agonizing tenseness, sweat pouring from him, his breath coming in choking gulps.

For a long time he lay motionless, until his strength returned and his tortured nerves got back to normal. Then he rose to his feet, rather shakily, and looked about him.

The first thing he noticed was that the floor of the bridge dipped sharply downward almost from the lip of the crevice.

"No going back that way," he muttered. "Never could get up enough speed running up the sag to clear the crack. Nowhere to go but ahead, and here's hoping this badger hole doesn't run up against a rock somewhere and stop. Well, here we go again!"

He groped his way down the steep slant, leaning against the gusts of wind, cautiously testing the ground ahead at each step. As he had surmised, the far end of the bridge led to a continuance of the tunnel. When he reached it he could just make out the darker opening yawning amid the shadows. Another moment and the giant wind and the wailing voices of the gulf were behind him.

For a while he proceeded cautiously, testing the ground ahead, but finally he grew too tired to care and plodded wearily onward, heedless of possible pitfalls, only taking the precaution to continuously brush one hand against the rock wall to anticipate the passage's devious windings. Once he heard the sound of rushing water nearby, but though he was parched with thirst he dared not attempt to reach it, for it evidently flowed some distance below the path he was following. He hugged the rock wall closely till the sound died out behind him. He was blind with fatigue when once again the premonitory grayness shaded the darkness ahead. He quickened his step, rounded a turn and stood dazzled by a bar of shimmering light which streamed across the corridor.

The light poured through an opening in the cave wall that rent the rock at about shoulder height. It was barely larger than a window.

Hatfield managed to scramble up to it, wormed his way through and found himself standing on a shelf of stone with a sheer cliff falling away at his feet to the floor of a canyon some sixty feet or so below. The far wall of the canyon, a half-mile distant, was ablaze with golden sunlight and the shortness of the shadows told Hatfield that the time must be somewhere around noon.

About a dozen feet below the edge of the opening, the cliff bulged outward, but beyond the rounded edge of the bulge he could see a gleam of water below. The water looked cool and inviting and he was conscious that his greatest desire was for one long drink.

He examined the cliff on either side of the opening. It was perfectly sheer. A lizard would have experienced difficulty negotiating a descent. He turned his gaze back to the water below. It looked deep but might easily be dangerously shallow. The rocky bank of the stream was but a few yards distant from the cliff base.

"If that happens to be Terloga Creek down there, I've got a mighty good chance of bustin' my neck if I try a jump," he told himself. "That darn freshet isn't more'n a couple of feet deep any place I've seen it. But that water does look a lot deeper. Let's see, now."

The height was not excessively great for a dive, but the bulge of the cliff presented a disquieting hazard. Should his body graze the bulge in the course of its descent, he would doubtless be hurled far enough out from the cliff face to miss the water and be dashed to death on the stones of the bank.

But once again he had scant alternative. The only one was to re-enter that dreary cave and continue his painful plodding along its winding burrow with the scant hope that another opening easier to negotiate might present.

"Nope, I've had enough of that darned hole," he muttered. "Here goes!"

Gathering himself together he leaped far out from the shelf's edge and shot downward through the screaming air. He grazed the cliff with scant inches to spare, struck the water with a sullen plunge and vanished.

Down, down he sank, until he thought he could never rise again, until his chest was bursting for want of air and waves of blackness were crowding down upon him. Then his feet touched bottom. He gave a mighty spring and began slowly to rise. He broke to the surface with a gasp of relief and gulped in great drafts of life-giving air. Then he began struggling toward the bank, which was only a few yards distant.

But the water was icy cold and the current ran like a mill race, with a tendency to sweep him back towards where the stream washed the perpendicular wall of the cliff with no beach between it and the water's edge.

Hampered by his clothes and his guns and weak with weariness, he swam sluggishly and for several tense minutes he hardly gained a foot. Then, with his strength rapidly failing and a feeling of numb disregard for consequences creeping over him, an eddy caught him and swirled him toward the far bank. A moment later his boot scraped on the gravelly bottom. Crawling and floundering through the shallows, he at last reached the stony beach and lay utterly exhausted.

Gradually the warmth of the sun beat the chill from his bones and revived his strength. He sat up, rested for a few moments; then tugged off his boots and emptied the water from them. He wrung out his clothes as best he could. His hat, held in place by the chin strap, was still on his head. He wrung it out, too, and batted it into something like its original shape. He gingerly felt of the still prominent lump on the side of his head where the gun barrel had landed.

"Lucky my old rainshed was on when they socked me," he muttered. "Sort of broke the force of the blow, I reckon. Just the same it must have been quite a wallop."

Feeling somewhat better, he donned his boots, got to his feet and climbed the steep bank to the canyon floor. He had not the least notion where he was and decided to follow the stream down-canyon.

The hot sun quickly dried his clothes and drove the stiffness from his limbs. After several miles of trudging, he reached a point where the perpendicular right wall of the steadily narrowing canyon gave place to a long slope not too steep to climb.

"On top of that, I should get some notion of direction," he reasoned and tackled the slope. After a tiresome climb he reached the crest and gazed about. He quickly realized that the hidden hangout was not in the western hills as he had supposed. To the south and west the smoke smudge that marked the site of Marton lay against the sky. He was somewhere in the hills that stretched across Webb Kenton's holding and old John Claibourne's Rafter C, that lay to the east of Kenton's Open Diamond range.

He found the fact interesting.

"And that darn creek I dived into must be the one that flows south across Arch Wagner's east pastures," he decided. "Well, if I head south by west a bit I should hit a trail before long. Anyhow that direction will take me to Marton sooner or later. Five or six miles of going, I'd say."

The sun was slanting into the west, but several hours of daylight still remained. After resting a bit after the climb, he resumed his weary trudging, working down the far slope in a diagonal. His high-heeled boots were not adapted to extensive walking and his feet were beginning to hurt. But he grimly kept striding ahead. After more than an hour of battling the sags and gulleys, he came out on a well-traveled trail that ran south. Here the going was better but it was nearly dark when at last he limped into Marton, deathly tired and famished.

Food was his first thought, so he headed for the Queen High. The outlaws had taken the small amount of cash in his overalls, but he had a reserve of folding money in the belt pocket that accommodated his Ranger badge.

When he entered the saloon he saw Sheriff Fulton standing in his customary place at the far end of the bar. The sheriff saw him come in and started. Hatfield wondered did he imagine it, or did Fulton's florid countenance turn pale. But if so, the sheriff quickly recovered his usual aplomb and waved a cheery greeting. Hatfield nodded in reply and sat down at a table.

"Now for a surroundin' that would founder a horse," he told himself as he beckoned a waiter,

After putting away a hefty serving, Hatfield felt much better. He bought tobacco and papers and smoked a couple of cigarettes. Tired though he was, he decided against spending the night in town. He left the saloon and headed for the livery stable. He did not know it, but he had barely passed through the swinging doors when Sheriff Fulton hurried out and made for Bascomb Price's office almost at a run.

Although he did not anticipate a second attack, Hatfield walked warily as he passed under the tree in front of the stable. Nothing happened. He paid Goldy's bill, got the rig on him and headed for the Open A.

When he arrived at the ranchhouse, a light was burning in the living room. Old Arch Wagner was still up. He greeted Hatfield with undisguised relief.

"Was gettin' bad worried about you," he acknowledged. "Where the heck you been? Your clothes look like you got caught in a thunderstorm, and how'd you get that bump on your head? Sit down. You 'pear tuckered. What happened, anyway?"

Hatfield sat down and told him. Wagner listened in silence broken only by his frequent oaths and ejaculations.

"Son," he said heavily when Hatfield had finished the tale, "Son, I'm going to give you some good advice. I hate to lose you, but the best thing you can do is fork that yellow horse of yours and ride fast and far. Those snake-blooded no-goods are after you, and if you stick around they'll get you. Sift sand, pronto. That's the best advice I can give you."

"Much obliged, but I'm not taking it," Hatfield smiled reply.

"Didn't figure you would," Wagner admitted, "but you'd oughta. Now get to bed. You look all in. We'll talk some more in the mornin'."

Hatfield took that bit of advice without arguing. He was asleep almost before his head hit the pillow. It was mid-morning when he descended to the living room. Old Arch was busy with some papers.

"Didn't see any sense in wakin' you," he said. "Feel better? I'll have the cook throw something together. Could stand a bite myself."

They had finished eating and were enjoying a leisurely smoke when a ranchman clattered up to the ranchhouse yard.

"It's John Claibourne of the Rafter C," said Wagner, craning his neck to look out the window. "What's eatin' that old coot? He looks like he's in a temper."

Claibourne was. He entered in response to Wagner's bellow to come in, growled an answer to the other's greeting and slumped into a chair.

"They took me for more'n a hundred head night before last," he announced without preamble. "Arch, this is gettin' plumb serious."

Wagner swore explosively. "You're darn right it is," he agreed with vigor. "Took 'em west as usual, I suppose."

"That's right," nodded Claibourne. "We tracked 'em across your north pastures and across the crik; but lost the trail on the black rocks at the foot of the hills, like we always do. We spent the whole day ridin' around in those cracks over there, and never did hit it again."

Wagner voiced a profane tirade against the rustlers, Claibourne adding his bit. Hatfield listened in silence, but with interest. Doubtless Claibourne's cattle were the "chore" the outlaws discussed while taking him to the hangout.

One thing struck him forcibly. It was clear that the mysterious Boss and his captors had contemplated taking part in the raid, but had announced their intentions to be back at the hangout the following morning.

"Which means they planned a pretty short drive," he mused.

"Certainly not through the western hills and down to Mexico. Looks like they must have a holding spot not far off. Now if I could only droop a loop on that spot."

He thought of the hangout as a clew to the holding spot, but reluctantly dismissed it. He was convinced that the hangout was to the south and east of the Open A, and Claibourne said the stolen cattle went west. It must be somewhere in the western hills. It would be simple to corral a herd in one of the many canyons until a favorable opportunity presented to drive it south to Mexico or west to New Mexico.

"That way they could wait till they got a big one together," he mused. "The setting is perfect. Those infernal lava beds that flank the hills on the east make it practically impossible to track a herd once it gets onto them. And the farmers' land west of the creek is bad enough. This thing is going to take some heavy thinking-out, and some smart moves."

Hatfield began to make his plans before the day was out. He rode down and paid Mose Brady a visit. The old farmer received him with marked cordiality. They talked a while about crops and local conditions. Suddenly Hatfield said, "Mose, I'd like to ask a favor of you."

"Anything I can do, son, anything I can do," the farmer assured him.

"You can do it all right," Hatfield replied. "And it won't inconvenience you in the least. I want you to allow the ranchers to patrol your unfenced lands up to the north. That will give them a much better chance to bust up the rustling that's plaguing them."

Brady stroked his beard thoughtfully. "Reckon you got somethin' there, son," he admitted. "I don't feel over kind toward the ranchers—guess I've got reason not to—but right is right and I'm willin' to help even a rancher to stop thievin'. Tell Wagner to go ahead. I'll vouch for the boys stringin' along with me."

Hatfield rode back to the Open A ranchhouse and informed

old Arch of Brady's decision. Wagner shook his head in bewilderment.

"I don't know how you do it, son, I don't know how you do it," he said. "I've a notion if you were of a mind to, you could talk a rattlesnake out of fangin'. I'll post some of the boys over there right away. I'll set 'em to ridin' patrol at the edge of those infernal lava beds."

Wagner did just that. And three nights later, the Open A lost more cows!

CHAPTER XII

THE RAGING WAGNER pulled everybody off the job, even the hands assigned to the important chore of getting a trail herd together for which the big Dawes ranch down by the Rio Grande was clamoring, needing the cows badly to fulfill certain contracted shipping obligations.

"I want every canyon in those hills combed to a finish," stormed Wagner. "I'm goin' to bust up this thing or go out of business tryin'."

"Not that I won't go out anyhow if it keeps up," he confided morosely to Hatfield.

From dawn till darkness the Open A hands put in a hard and tedious day, and accomplished exactly nothing. Jim Hatfield alone noted something he considered of significance, though just what it meant he still had not the slightest notion. He did not discuss his discovery with the others, not wanting to have his own thinking processes clouded by unprofitable theory and conjecture.

Once again he was convinced the stolen cows, or part of them, at least, had been turned back to the west bank of Terloga Creek.

Due to the high opinion Wagner and Happy Beeler had of his work, Hatfield was left largely on his own. He could govern his movements very much as he liked. Early the next morning found him on the banks of the creek at the point where the widelooped cattle had forded the stream.

For a long time he sat studying the broad, shallow sheet of hurrying water. He had a hunch that in some way Terloga Creek was the key to the mystery. Ultimately he rode slowly southward along the west bank, carefully scrutinizing every inch of the ground. Mile after mile he covered, until the tall ridge that shunted the creek westward was no great distance away.

"Looks like we're following a cold trail, horse," he told Goldy disgustedly. "I had a notion that maybe the sidewinders drove the herd down the creek for a ways in the water, where they'd leave no trail, and then shunted them west again. But so far there isn't a sign of a cow coming out of the water and heading across the range. Well, we'll amble along until this darn freshet dives into the ground on the chance of spotting something."

Another half-hour of slow riding and the creek turned westward in the shadow of the ridge. It ran straight and smooth for a mile or more, then abruptly it turned to the south. Five minutes more and Hatfield pulled rein before the high and wide mouth of a cave into which the stream flowed.

"Well, here it is," he mused, "and nothing accomplished."

Again he lounged comfortably in the hull, studying the water. From the cave mouth came a hollow rushing sound, similar to that he had heard while groping his way through the dark tunnel that led him from the outlaws' hangout to freedom. Suddenly he straightened up, the concentration furrow deep between his black brows.

"I wonder?" he muttered. "Sounds plumb loco, but I wonder. Horse, I reckon you'll figure I've gone looney as a tree full of centipedes, but we're going to take a little ride in the dark."

He sent Goldy down the bank and into the stream. Upon reaching the middle of the creek, the water of which did not come much above the sorrel's knees, he turned his head downstream and headed for the gloomy cave mouth.

Goldy didn't like it as the warm sunlight gave place to chill gloom that swiftly grayed to black darkness. He snorted his protest and shivered, but he kept going.

Hatfield's only emotion was one of intense curiosity. He knew that the sound of the water would give ample warning of a rapid or fall. There was nothing to fear from natural causes.

"But if my hunch is a straight one and somebody happens to be hóled up in here keeping watch, I may have plenty to worry about," he told himself.

He tried to estimate the distance covered, a difficult thing to do in the pitch dark and with the stream doing considerable winding. "A straight line of about three miles should do it," he mused, "but we're not following a straight line. Very likely it's considerably farther. But I sure don't want to come to the other end of this burrow without knowing it. That could be mighty interesting, if I'm figuring correctly."

Another twenty minutes and he slowed Goldy still more. The current seemed to have accelerated some—a sign, he reasoned, that he was approaching the point where the stream left its underground course. A little later he noted that the darkness ahead was graying. He pulled Goldy to a halt and dismounted.

"You stay put right where you are," he ordered, dropping the split reins into the water. "And keep quiet, too, darn you."

He was confident the intelligent animal would not move; anyhow he had to take the chance. To go splashing ahead on horseback would announce his approach to anyone who might be loitering around the exit.

The water came but little above mid-thigh and the current was not swift enough to sweep him off his feet. He forged ahead slowly, pausing often to peer and listen. The light was growing stronger, the sound of the water lessening, denoting that there was more room for the echoes to disperse. He rounded a shallow bend and halted, staring at an oblong of blinding sunlight. When his eyes had accustomed themselves to the change of light, he moved cautiously forward. A moment later he halted with an exultant exclamation. He was gazing through a wide opening from which the stream rushed. Directly ahead was a network of cunningly constructed dams. In one respect his hunch had proved a straight one. He was looking through the opening Webb Kenton blew in the cliff face to free the underground stream and provide water for his thirsty range.

Hatfield did not move out of the tunnel. To do so, he felt, would be foolhardy. If he was right in his long-shot surmise that the stolen cattle were run through the tunnel and out onto Kenton's range, anybody seeing him emerge from the tunnel mouth would very likely not be favorably impressed and apt to signify disapproval with the hot end of a bullet. He retraced his steps to where he left Goldy, mounted and turned the sorrel's head upstream.

"And now what?" he asked the horse. "I've proved that it would be possible to run a herd south through this hole, but that's all. If Webb Kenton is doing the widelooping and getting the stolen cows onto his range via underground Terloga Creek, what the devil does he do with them? From his holding the only way out of the valley is by way of Persimmon Gap, and only a plumb loco hombre would try to run rustled cattle south by way of the Gap. That trail is well traveled and a chance meeting with a bunch of punchers coming north after finishing a chore would be his ruination. He'd have to explain how he came to be pushing Open A and Rafter C cows south, and that would take considerable explaining. And of course I haven't the slightest proof Kenton is doing the stealing. I've just learned that it would be possible for him to do it, and that's all. Just as I suspect the same man who built the dams that control the released waters of Terloga Creek also built that cribbing which shallowed the water over the reef in the Rio Grande and wrecked the *Ranchero*. But again that's only suspicion. Not the sort of thing you take into court if you don't hanker to get laughed out."

Although not particularly afflicted by nerves, Hatfield was not as comfortable as he might have been during the ride upstream. His imagination, quickened by the echoing dark, conjured up all sorts of unpleasant possibilities. Suppose the rustlers had decided on a little daylight operation? Meeting them driving a herd south would be fraught with unwelcome consequences for himself. Still more disquieting, perhaps they used the tunnel as a short cut even when out on legitimate activities. They would doubtless consider his presence in the bore anything but legitimate, and would take appropriate steps to see that the visit was not repeated. He breathed deep relief when he ultimately reached the north end of the tunnel without incident. He studied the surrounding terrain before emerging from the gallery and rode out with every sense at hair-trigger alertness. Everything was peaceful so he turned Goldy's head toward home.

"We'll just give the boys on the north pastures a little hand with their combing," he told the sorrel. "Then tomorrow we got another ride ahead of us, and a ticklish one."

That night, however, a chance remark by Wagner changed Hatfield's plan of giving Webb Kenton's Open Diamond O range the once-over.

"Rustlin' or no rustlin', we got to concentrate on that trail herd for the folks down on the Dawes ranch," old Arch said. "They're raisin' hell for their beefs. They got government contracts and rely on us fellers up here to provide them with the surplus they need. Because of all the hell-raisin' we been fallin' down on 'em a mite and they don't like it. Can't blame 'em, and it's too good an outlet for our surplus for us to pass up. They pay top prices for stuff on the hoof and we don't have any shippin' charges. Just a straight drive south and, comparatively speakin', an easy one. Understand Webb Kenton is rollin' a herd tomorrow, better'n three hundred head, and that should ease things a mite till we get there with our big one."

"Starting tomorrow morning?" Hatfield asked casually.

"That's right," Wagner nodded. "I got it straight from Lafe Hartsook."

Before dawn Hatfield could be found riding swiftly for Persimmon Gap.

Shortly past where the trail, after a long and hard climb, dipped over the crest of the pass, he found a spot to his liking. Dense thickets flanked the trail on either side. Here the herd would be forced to proceed in almost single file. The cattle would be weary after the arduous climb and would proceed slowly till they caught their wind. The site was ideal for somebody wanting to get a good look at the brand marks.

Knowing he had plenty of time, Hatfield chose his post of observation with care. He holed up in a thicket from which he could see but not be seen. He took the precaution of tethering Goldy a considerable distance back from the trail, where there was little chance of his being heard even if he took a notion to kick up a racket, which was unlikely. These matters taken care of, the Lone Wolf stretched out on a bed of leaves, rolled a cigarette and took it easy.

It was well past noon when a distant bleating heralded the approach of the Open Diamond O herd. Hatfield took up his station at the spot he had selected and waited. Another half-hour and the cows began to file past his place of concealment, traveling at a shambling walk. Nobody rode point or swing, because the dense growth on either side of the trail would effectually prevent the cows from straying. This lessened the chance of his presence being observed.

Slowly the herd streamed past, at a distance of but a few yards, and there was not a brand on hip or shoulder that Hatfield did not see and mark. Finally the dust-powdered drag hove into view. Nearly a dozen hands made up the drag, a large number for a herd of less than four hundred head. Hatfield eyed them with interest. Some he had met in the course of his range work, others were unfamiliar. One big fellow with thick shoulders and a reckless, jovial countenance seemed to strike a chord of memory.

"Sure reminds me of the jigger who gave me a cup of coffee in that hangout," he mused. "Looks like what I figured he'd ought to. Born hell-raiser and a fellow who raised a bit too much and finally ended up on the wrong trail. Hmmm! Kenton doesn't 'pear to be riding with the herd. But then an owner often doesn't, especially on what's considered an easy drive. Well, there they go, and here I am, right where I started from."

He rolled a cigarette and swore in weary disgust. He hadn't missed a steer that shambled past his place of hiding, and each and every one bore Webb Kenton's Open Diamond O brand!

"Nope, no widelooped cows in that bunch, unless my eyesight's going back on me, and I don't figure it is," he told Goldy as he started on the long ride back to the home spread. "Looks like we've still got a bit of jumpy riding ahead of us."

The following day Hatfield had his hands full helping get the trail herd together, but the next found him riding wearily over Webb Kenton's Open Diamond O range. All day long he combed canyons and brakes and learned exactly nothing. Holed up in the brush atop a tall ridge, he watched Kenton's riders going about routine range chores and could detect nothing suspicious in their actions. He fervently wished he could discover the secret hangout, but had not the least notion where to look. All he knew was that an ascending trail led to it, perhaps up the wall of a canyon, and that it was located somewhere in the hills either on Kenton's holdings or on the Rafter C spread to the east.

The next day and the next he followed the same procedure, still with barren results. The terrain was a jumble of ridges, brakes and canyons. To comb them all would take weeks of intensive riding. On the third day he knocked off early and returned to the Open A ranchhouse before dark. That evening he sat by the open window and watched the full moon soar up above the eastern hills, bathing the rangeland with silvery light. Abruptly he stood up.

"May be a plumb loco notion," he muttered, "but I got a feeling this is a nice night for a little widelooping. Kenton's hands got back from the south today, Beeler said. Maybe that moon will inspire 'em. Anyhow, I'm going to play the hunch."

The ranchhouse was silent. The tired hands in the bunkhouse were evidently asleep. Hatfield got the rig on Goldy without disturbing anybody and turned the sorrel's head south by east. On a tall ridge crest from which he could see for miles in every direction over the moon-drenched prairie, he took his stand. Far to the northwest, dim with distance, he could see the towering elevation above the opening in the cliff face from which flowed the released waters of Terloga Creek.

"If my hunch is a straight one, something should come from that direction," he decided.

The hours passed slowly. Midnight came and went, and the prairie lay silent and deserted save for clumps of grazing cattle. Hatfield risked lighting a cigarette, and waited.

And then, when he was about ready to give up in disgust, he sensed movement to the north. At first it was but bouncing blobs flickering across patches of moonlight, vanishing into clumps of shadow, reappearing once again where the light was bright. As he watched, tense and eager, the objects resolved into cattle urged on at top sped by hard-riding horsemen. Soon Hatfield was able to count seven riders in all. There were nearly a hundred head of cows.

"Well, this looks something like," he muttered as the herd rolled nearer and nearer. "Nobody would have any legitimate reason for shoving a bunch along at that rate in the dead of night."

He waited until the herd swept past the ridge, then he rode swiftly down the brush-covered slope. When he reached the level ground, the herd was nearly a mile distant.

Hatfield followed, taking advantage of all cover that offered, devoutly hoping that the rustlers, if such they were, had no reason for keeping a close watch on their back trail. Apparently they did not, for, so far as Hatfield could ascertain, they never turned in their saddles.

Abruptly they veered the herd to the left, diagonalling it toward the continuance of the ridge, which now consisted of beetling cliffs below the upward flinging slope. A moment later Hatfield, watching closely, saw cattle and horsemen vanish into a dark canyon mouth. He pulled Goldy to a halt and studied the terrain. Across from the canyon mouth, after half a mile or so of open prairie, was broken ground grown with brush and trees. He waited a few minutes, then made a wide detour until he reached the shelter of the growth. He sent Goldy southward at a walk. The sorrel picked his way between clumps of brush and juts of stone until he was directly opposite the silent and apparently deserted canyon mouth. Here Hatfield pulled him to a halt.

Sitting his horse in the shadow, the Ranger debated whether to attempt to enter the canyon and decided against it. If he tried to ride across the open, moon-flooded prairie and somebody was watching from the canyon mouth, very likely the first intimation he would have of the fact was the tearing impact of a bullet. He stayed right where he was and schooled himself to patience.

The wait was long and tedious. Dawn was flushing the sky with rose and gold when the horsemen reappeared, riding out of the canyon mouth. Hatfield counted their number and heaved a sigh of relief. Seven men had entered the canyon. Seven men came out. It was logical to believe that there was nobody inside the gorge. He watched until the riders, speeding north by slightly west, had vanished behind the broken ground. Then he sent Goldy across the open prairie at brisk speed.

The ride through the fading moonlight was not easy on the nerves. If he had made a mistake and somebody was on guard, the results would be unpleasant, to say the least. However, he reached the canyon mouth without incident and rode into the gorge.

The canyon was narrow, not more than a couple of hundred yards in width at the mouth, and it rapidly narrowed still more. As the light strengthened, Hatfield saw that the north wall was perpendicular, the south a long slope that flung upward against a rounded skyline. And flowing steeply up the sag was a trail.

"And I'll bet it leads to that hangout," he muttered. "Chances are from up there they can get a view of the whole canyon. Sure hope there isn't somebody up there keeping an eye on things down here."

The thought was disquieting, but nevertheless he continued to ride up the narrowing gorge. Soon he saw that many cattle had passed that way. A broad trail was beaten out by their hoofs and by the irons of horses.

"This is it, I'm willing to bet a hatful of pesos," he told Goldy.

A moment later he heard the bawl of a steer no great distance ahead. He rode through a final fringe of growth and saw a stout corral fence that spanned the canyon, here little more than a hundred feet in width, from the northern cliffs to the steep slope on the south. And back of the fence were hundreds of cattle, some feeding or drinking from a little stream that gushed forth from under the cliffs, some standing placidly chewing their cuds.

Hatfield rode up to the fence and pulled rein. His glance swept over the scattered cows and he growled with irritation. Everywhere Webb Kenton's Open Diamond O brand met his gaze.

"Have I slipped up again?" he demanded aloud. Then his

eyes fell on a cow that was uneasily licking its haunch and the mystery was no longer a mystery. Hatfield stared at the cow, whistled under his breath.

"Well, I'll be damned!" he swore exultantly. "So that's it! And about as clever a job of brand-altering as I ever saw. If this don't take the shingles off the barn!"

CHAPTER XIII

THE IRRITATED cow bore the Open Diamond O brand, all right, but it hadn't worn it for long. High on its haunch were the familiar joined diagonals of Wagner's Open A brand. But below, freshly burned, was an Open A in reverse. And neatly circumscribed within the jaws was an O, also freshly burned. The composite result, a perfect Open Diamond O.

And a smooth piece of slick-ironing, Hatfield marvelled. A couple of weeks, with the scab fallen off and the hair blurring the edges, and nobody would ever notice how it had been done.

He dismounted and climbed the corral fence. Moving among the cattle he examined the brand of each. Every one had been altered, some of the burns were fresh, some a few days old, others a few weeks. He also discovered Rafter C brands as cunningly altered. Finally he went back to the fence, rolled a cigarette and pondered his discovery. Just what to do about it he was not at all sure.

Hatfield knew, of course, that when a brand is blotted or drastically altered, the change will show on the under side of the hide. Kill the cow and skin it and you have the evidence. Rather questionable evidence, however. Cow country juries have refused to accept it as conclusive. More than one case had been thrown out of court.

Here the "evidence" would be even more fallible. The slight

difference on the under side of the hide could result from an uneven pressure when the hot iron was applied to the hide. Of course, the fresh burns were damning. They would show conclusively that somebody had done a chore of brand-altering; but proving the act against Webb Kenton would be something else again. Kenton could plead ignorance of what some of his hands had been doing and doubtless make it stick. Said hands would conveniently trail their twine elsewhere. Hatfield shrewdly surmised that with Bascomb Price the judge, and Craig Fulton the sheriff, Webb Kenton pretty well controlled the country law enforcement machinery. Under such circumstances a case against him would have to be airtight. And what Hatfield had to offer at the moment was far from airtight.

"The only thing is to catch the thief red-handed," he decided. "And that's liable to require considerable 'catching.' Well, anyhow, now I know for sure who I'm twirling my loop for. Arch Wagner will go through the roof when he hears about this, and I'm scared it'll take considerable persuading to keep him from going off half-cocked and spoiling everything. Got a notion I can handle him, though."

With another glance around, he climbed the fence, swung into the saddle and sent Goldy back down the canyon. He was almost to the mouth when he swerved around a clump of brush and came face to face with a blocky, bearded man sitting his horse not twenty feet distant and with a gun in his hand. Even as Hatfield hurled himself sideways in the saddle, he fired point-blank at the Ranger.

Hatfield's quick move saved his life. The bullet missed its mark; but Hatfield was completely off-balance. His right foot flew from the stirrup and he fell. He grabbed frantically at the stock of his Winchester as he went down and jerked it from the boot. A bullet struck the ground so close it knocked dust into his face. Another ripped through the crown of his hat. Then the Winchester boomed sullenly and the man reeled in his saddle. Hatfield fired again and his enemy fell to the ground, a bullet laced through his heart.

Hatfield scrambled to his feet and leaped into the brush at the side of the trail. He crouched low, the cocked rifle ready for instant action.

But the silence of the canyon remained unbroken save for the snorting and stamping of the dead man's frightened horse. Hatfield waited a few minutes more then stepped back onto the trail. He eyed the dead man who lay sprawled on his back.

"And I got a plumb notion this is the hellion who wanted to plug me instead of taking me to the hangout that night," he muttered. "Well, he got his chance, but sort of slipped up. Now what the devil am I going to do with him?"

The body was indeed a complication. Left where it was for the fellow's companions to find, the whole business would be given away and like as not the wideloopers would seek cover. And that was the last thing Hatfield wished to have happen. After debating the matter for a moment he draped the corpse over his shoulder and carried it to the cliffs that walled the canyon on the north. He went through the fellow's pockets and discovered nothing. Then after considerable searching he found a suitable crevice and stuffed the body into it. He tumbled rocks into the crevice until nothing was to be seen.

The horse also posed a problem. It couldn't very well be hidden in a crevice, so Hatfield decided on the next best thing, to take the animal along with him and turn it loose a safe distance from the canyon. With good grass and water at hand, it was unlikely it would stray back to its home range, at least not for a considerable time.

He noted with interest that the trail up the slope began at the spot where the encounter had occurred.

"Chances are the hellion was headed for the hangout," he reasoned. "Must have heard Goldy's irons and got a bit suspicious as to who would be coming down the canyon. Lucky for me he didn't get more suspicious, otherwise he'd have likely holed up out of sight instead of sitting his horse in the middle of the trail. Then the chances are I wouldn't have known what hit me. Well, here goes." He speculated the trail up the slope, but decided that riding up it would be foolhardy. It could wait.

He gathered up the reins of the riderless horse. It trotted along docilely enough beside Goldy.

"Now if I just don't run into somebody," Hatfield muttered as he rode slowly from the canyon mouth, shooting keen glances in every direction. He located the canyon carefully in relation to certain landmarks for there was nothing to differentiate it from a dozen others slashing the granite breast of the hills. He drew rein for a moment before moving out into the brighter light and studied the nearby ridges and hilltops.

There was nobody in sight. Not likely to be this early in the morning. With a final glance around he headed straight east and rode swiftly till he was off Kenton's land and well onto John Claibourne's Rafter C range. Beside a waterhole where tall grass grew luxuriantly, he got the rig off the outlaw's horse. He hid saddle and bridle under a heap of brush. The horse was already contentedly grazing and would doubtless stay right where it was until somebody discovered it, most likely some of Claibourne's hands, who would either pass it up as not worth bothering with or take it to their home corral. In either case it was unlikely its former owner's companions would lay eyes on it very soon.

"They'll do a bit of puzzling over what became of that jigger but will hardly be able to figure out the truth, at least not until it doesn't matter," he decided. "Now we're heading for home and a gab with old Arch."

Wagner was sitting in the living room, gazing out the window when Hatfield arrived at the ranchhouse.

"Well," he growled, "and where the hell have you been? You seem to have more business than a toothpick merchant on Thanksgiving Day. Set down and take a load off your feet. The cook is throwin' something together. I ain't had breakfast yet."

Hatfield drew up a chair. He studied the old ranchowner for a moment and arrived at a decision. He took his Ranger badge from his belt pocket and laid it on the table.

Old Arch stared at the silver star set on a silver circle, but he did not appear as surprised as Hatfield thought he would be.

"Might have known it," he grunted. "You do things like a Ranger. So McDowell sent you down here, eh?"

"That's right," Hatfield nodded.

"Had any luck?"

"Some," Hatfield admitted. "I'll tell you all about it."

As the tale progressed, Wagner swore vivid oaths and wanted to confront Webb Kenton without delay. But Hatfield dissuaded him from impulsive action.

"We haven't really got a thing on him," he cautioned. "Nothing that would stand up in court, especially in a rigged court such as we'd very likely run up against in the county at present. Now I want to ask a few questions. First, what do you know about Webb Kenton?"

"Not a great deal," Wagner admitted. "As I told you before, he showed up here a couple of years back, not long after the nesters tooks over their land. Mentioned he was from Arizona, I believe. Nobody questioned that. Had no reason to. Folks in this section ain't in the habit of asking questions as to where a feller came from and what he did there. They take him on face value. Kenton has always showed up well. Sure he bested me in a deal, but that was just business. He's always behaved himself so far as anybody knows. Managed to keep on good terms with the cattlemen and the nesters both."

"And meanwhile he was doing everything he could, under cover, to stir up strife between the two factions," Hatfield interpolated. "One of the oldest owlhoot tricks. Go on."

"That's really about all I can tell you about him," Wagner admitted frankly. "As I said, he's always 'peared to be a squareshooter. Keeps to himself mostly, 'tends to his own business and is a first-rate cattleman. 'Pears to know all the angles."

"You can say that again," Hatfield agreed grimly. "Now how about Bascomb Price?"

"Price showed up here something under three years back," Wagner said.

"About the same time as Kenton," Hatfield commented.

"Four or five months before, I'd say," Wagner corrected. "He claims to be from California originally. I've a notion maybe he is. He had letters and papers showin' he'd been admitted to the Bar in that state. And he had a bank reference. One thing is sure for certain, he's a mighty able lawyer and a darn smart jigger in other ways. It was Price rigged the election against us. Never was such an upset."

"He and Kenton never appeared particularly friendly?"

Wagner shook his head. "Never seemed to pay any attention to each other. As I said, Kenton is good at keepin' to himself. His hands don't mix much, either. Price circulates around, but I don't rec'lect ever seein' him even talk to Kenton."

"And what about the sheriff?"

"He's been here a couple of years."

"*He* hit the section about the same time as Kenton did, eh?"

"Uh-huh, but there ain't nothin' mysterious about him. He's from over New Mexico way. Lots of folks around here knew him when he ran a saloon in Pantono, not far the other side of the state line. He came over here browsin' around and sayin' he was lookin' for a good investment. Bought the Queen High. Price took to eatin' and loafin' in the Queen High. Fact is, he did before Fulton took over. But lots of folks did that. It's always been about the best place in town and Fulton made it even better. He's a good saloon man and runs straight games. He's a mixer, like Price. That's how he come to run for sheriff, I reckon. Didn't take him long to get to know everybody. I've heard he loans the farmers money when they need some ready cash. Loans to the little cowmen, too."

Hatfield nodded, and considered what Wagner had told him.

"And it all adds up to practically nothing," he said. "If I had time to put Captain McDowell to the chore of tracing those fellows back to where they came from and getting a line-up on what they used to be and do, we might have something. But things are breaking too fast around here to risk taking the time. What I'm afraid of more than anything else is that something will tip my hand and they'll trail their twine. Once over the line into Mexico, they'd be safe, and all set to pop up someplace else with their hell-raising. And meanwhile the Scarlet Riders, of whom I'm convinced Kenton is the leader, aren't going to be sitting asleep in their hulls. They're liable to bust loose bad any time now."

"I would never have suspected Kenton of being mixed up in such a business," Wagner observed.

"No reason why you should," Hatfield replied. "If it hadn't been for two things—the little slip-ups such as the owlhoot brand always make—I doubt if I would have, either. At least not for some time. In the first place one look at those dams Kenton constructed convinced me that the man who designed them and the man who built the cribbing down on the Rio Grande were the same. Both showed more than average knowledge of the principles of engineering, and I consider it highly unlikely that two such gents would be mavericking around in a section at the same time. Secondly, something I promised Tommy Eden I wouldn't tell you, but under the circumstances I feel I'm justified in breaking my word."

He proceeded to relate the incident of the dynamited watch tower.

"Reckon I wouldn't have been overly hard on the young rapscallions," Wagner chuckled. "It was just a fool prank."

"Yes," Hatfield agreed, "but a prank that might easily have

had serious consequences. If they had been a bit closer when the dynamite let go, very likely one or more of them would have been blown to bits. That would have been enough to cause the friction between the cattlemen and the farmers to break into open warfare. Which was just what Webb Kenton hoped for. He's a snake-blooded varmint. Nothing would be more to his advantage, assuming that he really is the leader of the Scarlet Riders, than a rip-roaring wire war in the section. As I said, it's an old owlhoot trick. Get two law-abiding factions on the prod against each other. Then each goes to blaming the other for any hell-raising that goes on in the section, and they're too busy hornin' one another to concentrate on anything else. Which makes a perfect set-up for the owlhoots. That's what's been going on here to a certain extent. Kenton hoped to kick up a real row with his little scheme. It backfired through pure luck, and sure got me thinking seriously about him. In my own mind I'm convinced that he is the leader of the Scarlet Riders, and the man who killed Ranger Shafer in the course of the robbery of the Sunrise Limited up to the north and east of here. That's primarily my reason for being here. You don't kill a Ranger and get away with it."

Hatfield's eyes seemed to change color as he spoke. They were no longer the green of a sunny sea, but the cold gray of that same sea under lowering clouds. Looking at those terrible eyes and the grim set of jaw and mouth, Arch Wagner was ready to agree that killing a Ranger was bad business for the killer.

"The man who killed Shafer wore a scarlet mask," Hatfield continued, almost as if thinking aloud, "but it was agreed by all who saw him that he was a very tall man with broad shoulders. The fellow who was giving the orders down on the trail when I had the Terlingua gold wagon holed up in the brush was very tall, almost as tall as myself, I'd say, and had broad shoulders. I wasn't near enough to make out his features, but those things I noticed. Webb Kenton is a very tall man, and broad-shouldered.

Which tends to support my belief, to a certain extent. Wouldn't mean much if it were not for the corroborating evidence I have, but under the circumstances it means a good deal."

"I can see that," said Wagner. "You've got me convinced that Kenton, Price and Fulton are a nest of sidewinders that had ought to be tromped on, but the question is, as I gather, how in thunderation to do it?"

"Right now, I'm not sure," Hatfield admitted ruefully.

Wagner came up with a couple of suggestions. "Why not hole up where the creek comes through the cliffs and grab the varmint when he shoves the cows out onto his land?" he proposed.

"Would be all right, only very likely we'd just bag a few hired hands," Hatfield demurred. "It is highly doubtful if Kenton always rides with his men when they run off a few head. He's a slippery customer, and unless we got him dead to rights, the chances are he'd wriggle out of the loop."

"Wonder could we trick him into making a try for my trail herd—it's worth a heap of dinero."

Again Hatfield shook his head. "He's too smart for that," he replied. "That herd will run to about a thousand head. Why should he risk a desperate fight for what by his present methods he can run off in a week in comparative safety? If he got the herd, he'd have to send it tearing across the River into Mexico and then accept whatever somebody was inclined to give him for it. As it is, he just rebrands his stealings, waits till the burns heal and hair over a bit and then shove 'em into one of the herds he's disposing of and get top market prices for 'em."

Old Arch stuffed tobacco into his pipe and puffed furiously. Hatfield rolled a cigarette. As an afterthought, Hatfield showed him the deputy sheriff's badge from the pocket of the owlhoot he killed when he took over the Terlingua Mines wagon. Wagner examined it and 'lowed it looked like the ones worn by Deputy Chuck Davis and Bob Raines, who presumably departed for Arizona about the time the Scarlet Riders made their try for the Terlingua Mines gold.

"But I couldn't say more'n that," he admitted. "It just looks the same so far as I can see. I never noticed 'em particular. After all, sheriffs usually keep a few of these things on hand, for special deputies and the like."

Hatfield nodded and again they smoked in silence, Wagner scowling, the concentration furrow deep between the Lone Wolf's black brows.

A thought struck Wagner. "How about the spreads over east that have lost cows?" he asked. "The Tumblin' K and the Rockin' R, and the others. He couldn't change those brands."

"No, he couldn't change those brands into Open Diamond O's," Hatfield agreed. "That was where he was smart, and also where he slipped up. You and the Rafter C have been the big losers, haven't you?"

"That's right," Wagner nodded.

"Kenton would doubtless figure that if he stole only from the Open A and the Rafter C, somebody might tumble to the brand changing," Hatfield explained. "So he stole from everybody in the section. He didn't try to alter those other brands. Those cows he really did run on west and down to the "wet" market south of the Rio Grande, or over to the Reservation contractors in New Mexico. Where he slipped was in doing his cutting out west of Terloga Creek. That accounts for those prints coming and going west of the creek. And those prints heading back to the creek were what got me really thinking about the chance that he was running the cows south somehow."

Wagner nodded. They went on smoking in silence.

"By the way," Hatfield suddenly remarked, "you were telling me the other night about the Terlingua Mines planning to take over the Alhambra interests to the southwest of their property."

"Uh-huh," Wagner nodded. "From old Tom Lattimore. He's a character, that old coot. Owns the Alhambra lock, stock and barrel. We been dickerin' with him for quite a while and finally got him tied up. He wanted a hundred thousand, cash, but we finally talked him down to eighty. Says he'll dynamite the shaft before he goes any lower. He means it. Uh-huh, the deal is all but closed. The details will be ironed out in the next few days."

Hatfield looked thoughtful. "Eighty thousand dollars," he repeated, "and I suppose he'll insist on cash—hard money."

"You're darn right he will," Wagner grunted. "I told you he's a character. Don't believe in checks. Ain't got much use for banks, either, though I reckon he does keep most of his dinero in 'em. Why?"

Hatfield did not directly answer the question. He asked another of his own:

"Bascomb Price handled the Terlingua Mines legal matters, didn't he?"

"Uh-huh, for the past year and a half, since Galusha Hammer died. Of course, he don't any more. He give up private practice after he became a judge."

"But he would know about the Terlingua deal with The Alhambra?"

"Reckon he would," answered Wagner. "Papers were filed in his court, and so on."

Hatfield looked pleased. "So he'd know the deal is going to go through," he stated rather than asked. Wagner nodded, and gave the Ranger a curious glance.

"And even though Price doesn't handle private practice right now, it would not be particularly out of order for you, the Terlingua's biggest stockholder, to discuss the matter with him and perhaps ask for a little friendly legal advice."

"Guess not," Wagner agreed.

"And in the course of the talk you might let all the details of the business slip," Hatfield went on. "For instance you might mention the day on which Tom Lattimore will be paid his money, in the Terlingua offices, and that he plans to take the money home with him to the Alhambra, which I understand is several miles distant from the Terlingua holdings."

Wagner stared. "What in hell are you getting at, son?" he asked.

Hatfield did not answer. "Everything would be dependent on Lattimore's agreeing to work with us," he said slowly.

Wagner straightened in his chair. "By gosh, I'm beginning to get it!" he exclaimed. "Sure old Tom would work with us. He's loco as hell, but he's a squareshooter and he'd be glad to do anything that might tangle those snake-blooded owlhoots' twine for them."

"He would be taking a certain amount of personal risk," Hatfield observed. "It's a salty outfit, and as you said, snake-blooded."

"I reckon the only thing that ever scared Tom Lattimore was seein' his own face in a lookin' glass," Wagner declared with conviction.

"Then it might work," Hatfield said. "Eighty thousand in gold would be mighty tempting to an outfit like the Scarlet Riders. I've a notion losing out on that ninety thousand down by the river, that they thought was good as theirs, must have hurt. A fellow in Kenton's position has to keep the money coming in. Otherwise his men get restless and are liable to pull something on their own, fumble it and give the whole game away. Yes, if my deductions are correct and Price and Kenton are in cahoots, they'd very likely fall for it. We wouldn't risk the money, of course, on the chance of a slip-up, but that little item can be taken care of. A bag of iron-washers looks about the same as a bag of double-eagles, so long as the pucker string isn't drawn. Lattimore would be cautioned not to resist and to elevate pronto when he was told to. I don't think they'd shoot him just for the fun of it. What time would the money arrive at the Terlingua Mines office?"

"The stage bringin' it from the bank up to Chisos would pull in about seven o'clock in the evening," Wagner replied. "No danger of them making a try for the stage. It'll be loaded for bear, with double guards and outriders. Taking no chances."

"That will be fine," Hatfield said. "Then Lattimore would be leaving the Terlingua just about dark. The only catch in the scheme is where would they be likely to make the try? We have to figure that out."

"Shouldn't be hard to do," replied Wagner. "It's about five miles from Terlingua to the Alhambra mine town where Lattimore has his place. For better than four miles the trail runs across the open prairie, where you can see for a long ways on a moonlight night. But about a mile this side of Alhambra it runs through a belt of thicket for maybe an eighth of a mile. That would sure be the place for them to make the try."

"Looks that way," Hatfield agreed. "Well, what do you think? Shall we risk it?"

"Sure," answered Wagner. "It looks darn nigh foolproof to me. And when I get through talkin' to Bascomb Price, that buzzard will think he's already got that money in his pocket. I'll tell him everything Lattimore plans to do. Only hope he won't get suspicious."

"I hardly think he will," Hatfield said. "So far as I am able to judge, they have no reason to think I'm suspicious of them. I've a pretty strong notion they know I'm a Ranger or some sort of a peace officer. The way Price reacted the first time he saw me makes me believe that, but the chances are they figure they've pulled the wool over my eyes pretty well. We'll try to keep them thinking so. Be sure to keep those patrols riding in full view over by the lava beds. So long as they don't tumble to the fact that I know how they run off the cows, I think they'll feel pretty safe."

Wagner agreed. "I'll ride to town and see Price tomorrow," he promised. "Then I'll hightail over and arrange things with Tom Lattimore and the mine manager."

When Wagner returned from town the following evening, he was chuckling.

"I'm willin' to bet my last peso he fell for it," he told Hatfield. "That damn shyster was actually a-licking his lips when I'd finished telling him all about it. Tomorrow I'm headin' for Terlingua."

Could Hatfield and Wagner have been present at a meeting in Bascomb Price's office that night, they would not have been so complacent. Webb Kenton was there, and Sheriff Fulton and Deputy Chuck Davis. Fulton and Davis looked eager and happy as Price retold his conversation with Wagner and outlined his plan.

But Webb Kenton sat silent, brooding, his eyes darkening till they looked black.

"Well, what the hell's the matter with you?" Price demanded irritably. "Don't you like the set-up?"

"No, I don't," Kenton said flatly. "I think if we try to hold up Tom Lattimore we'll get nothing and very likely be blown from under our hats. Price, I believe that damn Ranger and Arch Wagner are setting a trap for us."

Bascomb Price raised both hands above his head and swore. Fulton and Davis looked scared.

"Yes, I smell a trap," Kenton repeated slowly; "but I've a notion we can outfox *Senor* Ranger and *amigo* Wagner. Now, listen."

As he talked, grins broadened on the faces of his hearers. Finally Bascomb Price said grudgingly, "Webb, I'll have to hand it to you—you're smart."

"With that eighty thousand and the cows we still have in reserve we'll be sitting pretty," Kenton said. "We can lay low for a couple of months till things cool down. That nosey Ranger won't hang around here forever, especially if nothing happens. And if he does, I'll figure a way to take care of him."

"He's the Devil himself," quavered Fulton. "He slides out of every trap we set for him easy as a greased snake."

"He won't slide out of the next one," Kenton predicted venomously. "The next time I'll handle things in person. There won't be any slip-up. You fools should have had enough sense not to go off and leave him alone in that mine. You might have known he'd figure some way out if he was left to himself."

"You should have told us that in advance," growled Davis. "You said to lock him up and then hightail to join up with you."

"Okay, it was a mistake all around," conceded Kenton. "But there mustn't be any slip-ups on this job."

"There aren't going to be," Bascomb Price announced decisively. "I'm going with you on this one. If I'd been with you down by the River we'd be ninety thousand to the good."

Kenton's thin lips curled. He grinned maliciously at Price.

"Say, if things don't work out right, it will sure be some haul for them, won't it? The judge and the sheriff and his chief deputy all in the same loop! That would be something!"

"That'll be enough of that!" rasped Price. "There ain't going to be any slips."

He glared at Kenton, but his gaze slid away from the derisive gleam in the dark eyes.

"Damned if I don't believe you'd get a lift out of it if it really happened," he grumbled.

"I would, except for one thing," Kenton admitted frankly. "I'd be there, too!"

CHAPTER XIV

ARCH WAGNER RETURNED from Terlingua in an exultant mood. "It's all set," he said. "Lattimore is rarin' to go and will do just as he is told. The money reaches Terlingua day after tomorrow."

"Then we'll ride for Alhambra tomorrow night," Hatfield decided. "We'll hole up in Lattimore's place during the day. You pick the hands we'll take with us. Ten should be enough. I'll swear them in as specials."

"We'll mow 'em over like settin' quail," Wagner declared.

"Maybe," Hatfield replied, a bit dryly. "I've had considerable experience with this kind of business, and it doesn't always work out the way you figure it; but I do think it looks pretty good. Worth a try, anyhow, and I'm darned if I can figure anything that looks better."

When they reached the projected scene of operations, Hatfield was pleased with the terrain. For miles the trail ran across fairly level rangeland. Then abruptly it turned into a belt of thicket. Tall growth flanked it on either side, thick enough to provide excellent cover in the dim light of late evening, but not so dense as to make moving about difficult. Through the east fringe of the growth ran a little stream. Cattle that dotted the range were moving about in the straggle, drinking from the brook or nosing the clumps of grass.

"That's in our favor," Hatfield remarked to Wagner. "Any

149

noise made will likely be attributed to those brush poppin' cows, which should help if we have to change our position. The layout is all to the good so far as we are concerned."

"And all to the good so far as they are concerned, too," Happy Beeler observed lugubriously. "Never saw a better settin' for a hold-up. This sort of a stick is liable to be hot at both ends."

Hatfield nodded sober agreement. He did not discount the advantages to the outlaws.

"Would be nice if they're already holed up here," a young puncher said nervously.

"Not likely," Hatfield returned. "They'd hardly show close to this place before dark."

"Pity we can't see 'em come," commented Wagner.

"It would help if we could, but we can't watch all ways at once and it won't do to split up our force," Hatfield replied.

"Where do you figure they'll pull it, if they do?" asked Wagner.

Hatfield glanced along the trail which ran arrow-straight through the growth for several hundred yards.

"The logical place would be up north near where the trail enters the growth," he decided. "We'll gamble on that. If they hole up farther down this way, we'll just have to skalleyhoot after them. It'll be much to our favor, of course, if we are close by when they make their move."

Not far from where the trail entered the growth they found an excellent spot to hole up. It was better than a hundred yards from the northern fringe and afforded excellent cover.

"If those cows over there would keep quiet, we could hear 'em come," Beeler complained querulously. "Every time one of those critters tromps on a stick I jump."

"Take it easy," Hatfield told him. "Now everybody keep quiet, and keep your ears open and your eyes skinned."

A tedious wait of more than an hour followed. Full night

descended and the darkness was intense. But not for long. The silver rim of the near-full moon appeared in the east and soon the prairie was flooded with ghostly light; but in the shadow of the growth the gloom was still deep.

Another half-hour, with the posse growing nervous, when Wagner whispered, "I hear horses."

"And wagon wheels," Hatfield added. "That should be Lattimore and his buckboard. Get set!"

Tense, vigilant, the posse listened to the click of hoofs and the grind of wheels as they approached. They strained their eyes toward where the trail flowed between the stands of dark growth, with a silver glimmer behind it like an opalescent curtain.

Suddenly the buckboard loomed against the curtain of light, grotesque and gigantic in the deceptive glow. It rolled forward swiftly. Now they could make out the shadowy form of the driver. As it came nearer and nearer, their nerves strained to the breaking point. It rattled past the hole-up, continued on its way down the gray ribbon of trail. Hatfield watched it dwindle away to the south, his face darkening.

"Come on," he ordered abruptly. "Out onto the trail and after that shebang. I think we're riding a cold trail."

They sent their horses forward swiftly. Another moment and the buckboard was beyond the belt of thicket. Hatfield increased the speed. They quickly caught up with the slower moving vehicle. Hatfield raised his voice in a shout. Lattimore turned on his seat, the moonlight glinting on his grizzled beard, and pulled up. A moment later the posse drew rein beside him.

"Not a thing happened," he replied to Hatfield's question. "Looks like you missed your throw, son."

"It does," Hatfield admitted. "We—"

"Listen!" Arch Wagner interrupted. "Don't I hear horses comin' from the north?"

"Get set!" Hatfield ordered. "Don't take any chances." He listened intently a moment.

"That's only one horse, and it's coming damn fast," he said. "Now what the hell?"

The speeding horseman flashed into view, came booming down the trail, waving his arms and shouting.

"Good God! It's Austin, the mine manager," exclaimed Wagner. "He's all covered with blood!"

The manager pulled his horse to a clattering halt and burst into a torrent of incoherent speech.

"Take it easy!" Hatfield admonished, gripping his arm hard. "Take it easy and tell us what happened."

The excited manager calmed somewhat. "They got the money," he panted, breathing in great gulps. "Lattimore hadn't been gone fifteen minutes when four masked hellions bulged into the office. We were putting the money in the safe. I tried to swing the door shut but one of them belted me over the head with a gun barrel."

"You were lucky," Hatfield said. "If they hadn't been afraid of rousing the miners, they'd have killed you. What happened next?"

"They tied us up, me and both the clerks," said Austin. "Half a dozen more came sneaking in. They gathered up the money and hightailed. We couldn't get loose till the night watchman came around and untied us. I grabbed a horse and headed this way fast as I could."

Profanity volleyed. Hatfield finally stilled the uproar.

"Outfoxed, that's all," he said. "They didn't fall for our yarn one bit, Wagner. But the hand isn't called till all the chips are down. Lattimore, take Austin home with you and put him to bed. The rest of you get set for a long ride. I've a pretty good notion I can guess where the hellions are headed for. All right, let's go—straight east across the prairie. Lucky we don't have to cross the hills down here, but we'll have to make it over those ridges on Kenton's southwest range. Let's go!"

"What you figurin', Jim?" Wagner jolted as they splashed through the stream and sped eastward.

"As I said, I'm pretty sure I know where they'll head for," Hatfield replied. "It's one of two places, the way I see it—Webb Kenton's ranchhouse or that hangout in the hills. I'm betting on the hangout; but either way, we'll have our chance. I figure they'll go there to divide the loot."

Hatfield set the pace. They rode at good speed but did not push their horses.

"I don't figure there's any hurry," he told Wagner. "They have a head start and they won't run their cayuses to death. Besides we don't want to overtake them in the open. Some of them would very likely give us the slip if we did, perhaps the ones we want most. We'll try to catch them settin'. And that will be in their hangout. We're in for a fight no matter what happens. I doubt if Kenton or Price will be taken alive. So get set for business."

Mile after mile flowed under the horses' hoofs. The moon swung across the sky. The darkness deepened as it sank lower and lower in the west. The horses toiled up the ridges on Kenton's south range, jolted down the sags, tackled more slopes. Finally, after a last descent, a dark canyon mouth yawned before them.

"This is it," Hatfield said. "The trail runs up the south slope. I think I can pretty well judge the distance to that mine tunnel from where it begins. Let's go!"

They paced their horses slowly up the winding trail, pausing from time to time to listen. Where a bristle of growth encroached on the track, Hatfield called a halt.

"We'll leave the horses here," he decided. "Can't take a chance of going clicking over the rocks any farther. If they hear us coming we'll very likely get a hot reception. We want to be all over them before they know what's happened. Chances are there's about a dozen of them and that makes the odds even. It's up to us to get the jump."

Silently as wraiths they stole forward on foot. They rounded a final bulge high up above the canyon floor and found themselves on a little mesa. Directly ahead loomed the dark bulk of a cliff. At its base was a gleam of light.

"They're in there, all right," Hatfield breathed. "That door opens out. If we can just make it to the door and swing it back, we'll have the advantage. Let's go, and for Pete's sake don't make a sound!"

It was ticklish work, stealing across the open space. Should somebody be on watch outside, *they* would be the sitting ducks. They reached the doorway. Hatfield gripped the heavy hasp that swung loose and flung the door open. The posse boiled in, narrowing their eyes against the light.

Seated around the table, that was covered with gold pieces, were a dozen men. Webb Kenton was facing the door, Sheriff Fulton on one side of him, Bascomb Price on the other. Hatfield's voice rolled in thunder:

"Hands up! In the name of the State of Texas! You're under arrest. Anything you say—"

Webb Kenton, his face bleak with rage, yelled a curse and surged to his feet, hand streaking for his gun. The others came erect. The table went over with a crash.

Hatfield's Colt boomed sullenly. A lance of light gushed from its muzzle, seemed to center on Webb Kenton's broad chest. The outlaw leader fell, writhing and jerking. The rock walls quivered to a roar of gunfire.

Back and forth through the swirling smoke wreaths, jets of fire spurted. The bellow of the guns, the shrieks and yells, the cries and groans of wounded men blended in one horrific bedlam of sound.

In scant seconds it was over. Bodies lay around and over the table. Five men were backed against the wall, their hands in the air, howling for mercy.

"Hold it!" Hatfield shouted to his companions. "Grab those hellions and tie 'em up. If they make a move, let them have it." He strode forward, his guns still smoking. Abruptly he holstered one and plucked the silver star from his breast. He leaned over and held the symbol of law and order before Webb Kenton's glazing eyes.

"Even up for young Tom Shafer, Kenton," he said.

Webb Kenton's lips moved in a last vindictive curse. He stiffened, fell back and was still.

"Here's Bascomb Price with a hole between his eyes!" somebody shouted exultantly. "And here's Chuck Davis. There's a hole through his deputy sheriff's badge. And look, there's a cigarette, still burnin', hanging from his lip."

"And here's Craig Fulton with a busted arm," said Arch Wagner. "Come and look him over, Hatfield, he's a prize specimen."

Hatfield strode over to the moaning, fear-crazed sheriff, and looked him up and down with cold eyes.

"It'll take a stout rope to bust your fat neck, Fulton, but I reckon we'll find one strong enough," he observed cheerfully. "Ready to talk?"

Fulton instantly burst into a torrent of speech.

"He tied up the loose ends for us, all right," Hatfield agreed with Arch Wagner. "Price was really from California. He worked with Kenton over there and got himself disbarred for crooked work in land deals. Was headed for the penitentiary when Kenton and his bunch helped him break jail and get away. They made their getaway to New Mexico and holed up there a couple of years, working at smuggling and widelooping cows across from Arizona. When it got too hot for them there, they decided to move farther east. Price scouted ahead and picked the Big Bend country. He sent for Kenton and the others. They brought Fulton in and a couple of his off-color bunch. Kenton knew Fulton before he set up in business in New Mexico."

"A prime bunch of sidewinders, all right," growled Wagner.

"Yes," Hatfield agreed. "Kenton was smart and with considerable education. But he couldn't stay straight. And of course his bunch insisted on easy money. Price wanted to go slow and build up inside the law. If Kenton had agreed he might have done well by himself and the others. But Kenton couldn't see it and Price had to string along with him. They finally worked up a nice system. With Price as a lawyer and then a judge, it was easy for them to get the lowdown on anything going on in the section, like the Terlingua gold shipment and the like. Smart, but not smart enough."

"Not smart enough to buck the Lone Wolf, anyhow," chuckled Wagner.

"I got the breaks," Hatfield smiled. "Well, we'll patch up the boys—nobody seems to be seriously hurt—and head for town. Reckon we'll have to round up a few new county officials before we can get down to business. Sort of made a clean sweep of the old bunch."

The prisoners were taken to town and locked up. Hatfield, Wagner and Charley Bennet, the judge defeated by Price for re-election, held a conference.

"We are sort of short of county officials," Wagner remarked. "Charley here will accept the appointment and fill out the term as judge, but I don't know what we'll do about a sheriff. John

Snyder is sick—they say he has Bright's disease—and it's doubtful if he'll get well."

"I've a suggestion to make," Hatfield said. "Why not appoint
Moses Brady, the head man of the farmers. He'd make a prime
sheriff and it would help all the factions to get together. And I
figure young Val Carver would make a good chief deputy. That
would please the little owners."

Wagner looked startled, and for a moment resentful. Then he
chuckled.

"Hatfield," he said, "I believe you've got something there.
You've already convinced me that our row with the farmers is
nothing but damned foolishness. We'll ride up and talk to
Brady."

An astonished man was Moses Brady when Hatfield and
Arch Wagner rode up to his farmhouse. At first he was hesitant,
but he finally agreed to accept the appointment.

"Won't have any trouble fixing it with the Commissioners,"
Wagner assured him. "And there's something else I want to
talk to you about. Us fellers have got to get together. We've just
finished seein' what fightin' among ourselves leads to. The cowmen can use the stuff you fellers raise over here. That forage will
come in mighty handy in the wintertime. No sense in shippin'
it out of the section. And you'll need more good land to raise
all the stuff we'll need. That strip of mine east of the creek will
grow stuff fine. I'll lease it to you on your own terms. Also, you
ought to have modern machinery. I got some spare cash I'll advance for proper equipment. Oh, shut up! I ain't doin' nobody
a favor. I'm just makin' a good investment. We're goin' to make
this section the best in Texas. Shake on it, Brady!"

The two old men shook hands, smiling.

Jim Hatfield also smiled.

He rode away the following morning, his eyes sunny. He

had come into a section torn by strife, turmoil and hatreds. He was leaving it peaceful, contented, looking to the future. With the rising sun a golden flame to light his path, he rode on, an expression of pleasant anticipation on his sternly handsome face, to where danger and new adventure waited.

THE END

Leslie Scott was born in Lewisburg, West Virginia. During the Great War, he joined the French Foreign Legion and spent four years in the trenches. In the 1920s he worked as a mining engineer and bridge builder in the western American states and in China before settling in New York. A bar-room discussion in 1934 with Leo Margulies, who was managing editor for Standard Magazines, prompted Scott to try writing fiction. He went on to create two of the most notable series characters in Western pulp magazines. In 1936, Standard Magazines launched, and in *Texas Rangers*, Scott under the house name of **Jackson Cole** created Jim Hatfield, Texas Ranger, a character whose popularity was so great with readers that this magazine featuring his adventures lasted until 1958. When others eventually began contributing Jim Hatfield stories, Scott created another Texas Ranger hero, Walt Slade, better known as *El Halcon*, the Hawk, whose exploits were regularly featured in *Thrilling Western*. In the 1950s Scott moved quickly into writing book-length adventures about both Jim Hatfield and Walt Slade in long series of original paperback Westerns. At the same time, however, Scott was also doing some of his best work in hardcover Westerns published by Arcadia House; thoughtful, well-constructed stories, with engaging characters and authentic settings and situations. Among the best of these, surely, are *Silver City* (1953), *Longhorn Empire* (1954), *The Trail Builders* (1956), and *Blood on the Rio Grande* (1959). In these hardcover Westerns, many of which have never been reprinted, Scott proved himself highly capable of writing traditional Western stories with characters who have sufficient depth to change in the course of the narrative and with a degree of authenticity and historical accuracy absent from many of his series stories.